A RUSSIAN IN BERLIN

Alexander J. Motyl

Quamquam Quidquid Press

ISBN-13: 9798766292579
ISBN-10: 1477123456

Cover design by: Art Painter
Library of Congress Control Number: 2018675309
Printed in the United States of America

CONTENTS

A RUSSIAN IN BERLIN
Alexander J. Motyl

CHAPTER ONE

Professor Serge Romanoff arrived in West Berlin on Monday. He delivered the keynote speech at a conference commemorating the end of World War II on Tuesday. An interview, along with some photographs of him, appeared in the *Berliner Zeitung* on Wednesday. On Thursday, all hell—a word one uses with great caution in post-war Germany—broke loose. Five women, ranging in age from forty to seventy, accused him of having raped them thirty years ago, in the summer of 1945, when the Soviet army stormed Berlin and, not incidentally, systematically violated well over a million defenseless German *Frauen*.

Outraged, flustered, and confused, the Ivy League's leading Russian historian heatedly denied the accusations and insisted he was the target of a right-wing conspiracy aiming to discredit Russia and its liberation of Nazi Germany and to rehabilitate Nazis by painting them as victims of the war they had started and conducted with utmost brutality in the occupied Soviet territories. That the accusations appeared in a large-type newspaper belonging to Axel Springer, the anti-Communist German publisher detested by the liberals and the left for his conservative sympathies, lent credence to the professor's denials. That the women volunteered to appear before the public at a press conference lent credence to their accusations. Complicating matters were the inconsistencies and contradictions that emerged in *Rashomon*-like fashion in the women's accounts, as well as in Romanoff's, and were compounded in no small measure by the Janus-faced personalities of all the main players in this occasionally tawdry melodrama.

By the time the weekend rolled along, that admittedly

small part of West Berlin's public opinion that followed the controversy split into two polarized camps more or less coterminous with the traditional division into left and right. Critics of the women claimed they were at worst Nazis, at best sympathizers of the Hitler regime, intimating that the ladies, like the Germans in general, got what they deserved. Critics of the professor hinted at his being an unrepentant Stalinist with a cushy job at Harvard, a violent, lecherous monster who preyed on defenseless womenfolk amid the smoking rubble of post-war Berlin. Romanoff himself, although scheduled to return to his awe-struck students and fawning colleagues on Sunday, decided to extend his stay indefinitely, figuring he'd be better off settling the matter as soon as possible, before it made headlines in America, and hoping to demonstrate that his decision to stand and fight should be construed as proof of his innocence.

*

Summer was officially over—although the canals still sparkled with flocks of crystalline butterflies when the sun hit them at just the right angle—and Berlin was set to plunge into the unrelieved grayness of two wet seasons of Teutonic angst amply leavened with premonitions of a Wagnerian *Götterdämmerung*. Bonn, West Germany's political capital, was cheerful in comparison, combining the reassuring familiarity of a small town with the old-world stuffiness of political elites who were less powerful than they wanted to be and more powerful than they comfortably were. Frankfurt, the country's economic capital, was depressingly single-minded in its pursuit of lucre, but it vibrated with existential vitality—perhaps because the student radicals who dominated the university never let the capitalist barons forget just how precarious their hold on law and order —and, thus, on being—was. In contrast, West Berlin was an island of the doomed, consisting of too many theatres, too many operas, and too many museums, all trumpeting their superiority over the malnourished and malfunctioning East, while desperately hoping to persuade an indifferent world that the Prussian capital and the seat of the Hohenzollerns was more than a city of refugees, squatters, radicals, guest workers, and limbless men and dowdy women who had seen too much and wanted to blot it all out of their minds.

It was also the city where the last war had officially ended and where several more wars were still being fought. There was, above all, the Cold War. Its front line was the Wall, *die Mauer*, which kept the gum-chewing Americans and vodka-swilling Soviets at arm's length—well, except for that brief tank stand-off in 1961—and was the only thing that stood between the decrepit East German Communist regime and collapse. All the major spy services of North America and Europe had their agents in Berlin, where they mostly performed routine bureaucratic tasks, kept abreast of one another's goings-on, and occasionally engaged in dramatic exploits. Once in a while, some Russian or Ukrainian or Belorussian émigré would be kidnapped by the Communists or found dead in his bathtub or in some staircase; once in a while, some East German or Russian diplomat would mysteriously disappear, only to reappear a few months later with a broad grin and large bank account in suburban Virginia.

There was the war that the *Vertriebenen*, or German expellees from Eastern Europe, waged against both communism and their own insufficiently anti-communist government, demanding the right to return to cities, towns, and villages that would have struck them as foreign had they succeeded in resuming their interrupted lives. The squatters—mostly penniless students, who hoped their ramshackle communes would be forerunners of true socialism, true anarchism, or some other anti-capitalist, anti-imperialist utopia—fought a war against the Berlin authorities who, technically, were subservient to the four Allied occupying powers, and not Bonn. They seized run-down buildings with leaky indoor plumbing, rusty water, and clogged toilets, often in depressed areas near the Wall, spray painted all manner of colorful liberationist slogans on their gray exteriors, and refused to pay rent, knowing that officialdom, indifferent to the fate of the slums, would look the other way. Finally, there was the shooting war—in fact, the only conflict employing real violence—between the revolutionaries above and below ground and their *bête noire*, the German capitalist state. Berlin was a magnet for West Germany's radicals, who could, thanks to its special status, avoid the draft, grow their hair long, and engage in the untrammeled pursuit of revolution.

The Red Army Faction did not conceal its insurrectionary goals or its dedication to violent means. Their theoretician, the dark-haired, innocently round-faced Ulrike Meinhof, had joined the anti-nuclear movement while a student at the University of Münster. In 1959 there followed membership in the Communist Party of Germany. Ten years later, as civil protests, revolutionary movements, and armed uprisings swept the globe—from Uruguay to Selma to China—she opined, in an odd combination of solipsism and social conscience, that "Protest is when I say this does not please me. Resistance is when I ensure that what does not please me occurs no more." That was the first step from theory to practice. In 1970, she abandoned her family and formally left the world of bourgeois legality for the proletarian underground. It was then that she penned an essay that would inspire her comrades as well as thousands of German students, "The Concept of the Urban Guerrilla." Her own guerrilla days were all-too-brief, however, and in 1972 she was captured, sentenced, and interred in a notorious maximum-security prison in Stammheim, where she was joined by the other two key players in the RAF—Andreas Baader and Gudrun Ensslin.

The rakish Baader was more of a thug with a swagger than a revolutionary with a program. He had dropped out of high school, gravitated toward the left-wing student scene in Berlin, reinvented himself as a self-styled revolutionary, firebombed a store or two in Frankfurt to prove the point, trained with al-Fatah in Jordan, and then, in what his comrades had to consider a major anti-climax, was captured. Just what the strikingly attractive Ensslin, the daughter of an Evangelical pastor who had dispatched her to high school in the heartland of America, Pennsylvania, saw in Baader isn't clear, but they became lovers—after she left her husband, Bernward Vesper, the tortured son of a Nazi poet who lost his mind and took his life—and, for a while, lived a kind of Bonnie and Clyde existence before being arrested. As far as Ensslin was concerned, West Germany was fascist and violence against fascism was perfectly justified, indeed obligatory. After all, it was precisely because Germans were too unwilling to employ violence in 1933 that Hitler was possible—a point that even her most severe critics had to acknowledge as having some validity.

Ironically, although Meinhof's name was always linked with Baader's, the RAF was far more the brainchild of the two women than of the intellectually lightweight ex-hooligan and attracted more women than men—or at least as many—a fact that confused the West German police, which, like most unimaginative police forces, was accustomed to dealing with male criminals. The women who joined or supported the RAF were, evidently, committed to change at all costs, even though most of them, like Meinhof and Ensslin, hailed from solid middle-class backgrounds and should, in principle, have had nothing to complain about in a Germany that had just experienced an economic miracle in the 1950s. Some Germans observed that the women revolutionaries had betrayed such traditional female virtues as gentility, restraint, and kindness. Others insisted that the preponderance of women in the Baader-Meinhof gang proved that women, like men, were killers at heart. Still others resolved, sadly, that what had been proven was that *German* women, like German men, were killers at heart.

*

The leaders of the RAF were under lock and key as Romanoff arrived in Berlin, but the underground movement they had founded—abetted by several thousand above-ground sympathizers who provided the revolutionaries with food, shelter, clothing, and transport—was vigorous and resilient, resisting penetration, capture, and disbandment. Was it a premonition of things to come that, one day before his arrival at Tegel Airport, a bearded young man of possibly Arabic origin had been arrested on the terrace of one of the terminals with a bazooka in his duffel bag? He claimed to have mistakenly taken the elevator to the wrong floor, but, after he began to run and extracted a pistol from his side pocket, the police shot first and he was killed. The RAF distributed a statement expressing solidarity with the man and the third world struggle against capitalism, fascism, and imperialism. So, too, did a little-known splinter group, the Revolutionary RAF.

Security at the airport was especially strict that day and it was small wonder that the customs agent pursed his lips, squinted, and carefully scrutinized the nattily dressed American with a Russian name and surname before finally stamping his passport. His suspicions may have been aroused by Romanoff's untimely riposte to his routine query about the purpose of his visit: business or pleasure? Romanoff's remark, that "there can be no pleasure in Berlin," was not inaccurate, at least in comparison to London or Paris, but, as he realized as soon as he said it, needlessly provocative. Although he mumbled a muted apology, the agent's mood remained sour and he flipped the passport back at Romanoff, who dropped, and then had to stoop to retrieve, it.

In what poets might have interpreted as the city's taking its sweet revenge, Romanoff's taxi had a flat tire on the way to his hotel, the Kempinski. Adding insult to injury, the explosion produced by the bursting tire momentarily threw him into a panic. Jet-lagged and disoriented, he imagined that the swerving vehicle was under terrorist attack and dived to the floor of the cab. The bemused driver, a large Turk with a drooping coal-colored handlebar mustache, said something that sounded like "It is only tire, Efendi," and, sliding the wounded taxi to the side of the road, hurriedly whispered a brief prayer and proceeded to replace the bad tire with an even older one with no threads. He drove slowly. When they pulled up to the hotel one hour later, Romanoff instructed the potbellied bellboy to take his suitcases, headed straight for the bar, and, after downing a double scotch in one delicious gulp, approached the reception in better spirits, even engaging in some flirtatious banter with the petite brunette who took his passport, and registered. His suite, on the ninth floor, faced the back and was mercifully free of any traffic noise. The bellboy, seemingly preoccupied with polishing a vase with his tie, quickly vanished upon receiving a ten-mark tip.

As Romanoff expected, the conference at the Free University was uneventful and went according to script. Some fifty people drifted into a sloped auditorium that could easily have accommodated three times the number; most sat in the back, while the organizers occupied the seats in the front rows before the curved table, fold-out chairs, and a podium with a microphone. The morning panel featured three German scholars who focused on Hitler and the Nazi regime. One Brit, one Frenchman, and two Russians comprised the afternoon panel and they discussed the Allied liberation of Germany in general and Berlin in particular. Conveniently, the Cold War was not on the agenda.

As usual, Romanoff, like everyone else, knew exactly what the speakers would say, just as they could guess what wisdom he would impart in his keynote. Since several Soviet diplomats and scholars were officially in attendance (just how many spies were unofficially in attendance was unknown), his role was to be conciliatory, forward-looking, and irenic, so he talked briefly about his life, his research, and the great strides scholars had made in promoting mutual understanding and peace. The speech was boilerplate, but the Germans applauded long and loudly, if only because anything that offered an alternative to the daily barrage of depressing news about the Baader-Meinhof revolutionaries and their determination to destroy German *Gemütlichkeit* was welcome. If that anything also reinforced regnant self-understandings of German war guilt and Russian virtue, all the better.

The Soviet diplomats, all with hairless pates, all attired in the baggy gray suits favored by the Politburo and its tailors, and all wearing impeccably shiny shoes that squeaked, approached Romanoff during the cocktail reception and offered their hearty congratulations for his *"otlichnaya rech."* The speech was anything but exceptional, but Romanoff, who was temporarily thrown off balance by the contrast between the dowdy Soviets and the statuesque blonde who accompanied them and now stood, arms akimbo, facing him, knew better than to question the protocol, so he returned their oily smiles and made another toast to peace.

"*Vy govorite po-russki?*" one of the Russians asked with surprise.

"*Da*, I do speak Russian," Romanoff answered, though a tad reluctantly. Was the meeting accidental—he had learned years ago that there were no accidents or coincidences in Russia —or were the Soviets trying to draw him into their net again?

"Then," the diplomat continued in Russian, "we will not need the services of this lovely girl. *Eta devochka*—this girl— is *Fräulein* Eichendorf, our translator." A gold tooth glistened proudly between his wet lips. "She is as talented as she is beautiful." The other two joined in his laughter.

Exuding a sovereign indifference to the Russians' smirks, Eichendorf, wearing faded bell-bottomed jeans and sporting bangs that almost succeeded in hiding her penetrating eyes, extended her muscular hand and, while shaking Romanoff's, threw back her head, revealing two almond-shaped nostrils. Then, completely unruffled by the presence of a Harvard genius, she coolly remarked, "Another Russian in Berlin? *Nu, nu, nu. Willkommen.* Soon we Germans will be outnumbered—*Gott sei dank*—thank God." Feeling unnerved by her hard-edged demeanor, Romanoff withdrew his hand from her grip, excused himself, and, after dropping a score of *Auf Wiedersehen*'s, made for his hotel, relieved to be beyond Eichendorf's grasp and the Russians' grins.

Romanoff usually declined invitations to such ritual happenings, but a not inconsiderable honorarium, a prepaid business class seat with unlimited champagne and a tolerable filet mignon, a decent room in an elegant hotel, and the opportunity to meet some old contacts in Berlin proved decisive. It almost goes without saying that, when all hell broke loose that

Thursday, the professor sincerely regretted having succumbed to the temptation of a brief sojourn in *Schlaraffenland*. In Pieter Breughel the Elder's promised land of sloth and plenty, the sated peasants lay sleeping, oblivious to the rest of the world. Not so with him, alas. He should have known that Berlin could be as unkind to a Russian as Russians could be unkind to it.

*

The vehemence of Romanoff's denials reeked of sincerity, but, as he knew, they rested on slightly, and perhaps even dangerously, thin ice. The matter would have been instantaneously settled if he had never been to Berlin. Alas, he had served in the Soviet armed forces that liberated the city in 1945. A dedicated member of the Young Communist League, the Komsomol, he had enthusiastically volunteered in the summer of 1944, when the Soviets were on the verge of expelling the Wehrmacht from the USSR, and, after minimal training in a makeshift camp, had been given a gun, knapsack, uniform, boots, and helmet and sent to the front in Poland. He had encamped on the eastern bank of the Vistula River and, after waiting for the Germans to crush the Warsaw Uprising, took part in the progressive seizure of the Reich's dwindling territory.

It was then that the rapes began, as the German inhabitants of Prussia and the grain-growing Juncker lands that were eventually ceded to Communist Poland fled in anticipation of Soviet reprisals. Romanoff, then a shaveless fifteen, had been shocked by the sudden transformation of the master race into a ragtag bunch of terrified women, bawling children, and white-haired men. Unfortunately, their younger men folk put up a fierce resistance that cost much Russian blood before the red flag finally flew triumphantly from the Reichstag and the Germans had unconditionally surrendered in Karlshorst.

It was then, in mid- to late May 1945, that, according to the newspaper, the five women insisted that a tall, blond-haired boy had attacked them at night, as they were rushing to whatever remained of their homes, and violently raped them. The women claimed not to have known one another before the professor's interview. Each one had, after reading it, contacted the Springer paper in the hope of getting some publicity for her case. It was the newspaper or, more exactly, one of its star reporters, Sieglinde Bollow, who collected their stories and produced the bombshell that led to Romanoff's extended stay in Berlin.

He had been to Berlin, both West and East, many times since the end of the war and he had given many lectures, in his charmingly accented German, at both the West's Free University and the East's Humboldt University. There had also been interviews, mostly in low-circulation local papers and a few left-wing broadsheets, and one longer story in the Communist Party's official organ, *Neues Deutschland,* which lauded him for presenting a view of Russian history that "objectively" corresponded to that taught by Soviet ideologues and historians. Romanoff's American colleagues had teased him about the piece and the dean, with a twinkle in his besotted eye, had even asked if he had decided to join the Reds.

In fact, it was back in 1949, when he had been stationed in one of East Berlin's malodorous army barracks, that Romanoff had decided to cross over to the West. His motives, as he later told the American authorities, had not been political. True, the air lift of 1948-1949 had impressed him with its efficiency and organization; and, true, too, a clandestinely acquired copy of *Look* magazine had exposed him to the charms of American womanhood. But, when Romanoff, then nineteen years old, decided to violate the line of demarcation and say good-bye— *do svidaniia!*—to the Soviet Union and Stalin, he did so, as he later stated, because he wanted to "see the world" and "get an education at Cambridge," which he heard had left-wing leanings compatible with his own. The Soviets insisted he had been kidnapped by the Americans, bound and gagged, and transported to the capitalist West. Curiously, Romanoff never denied that charge; neither did the Americans.

Nothing came of *that* Cambridge, but, after a few years in Berlin doing odd jobs and learning a variety of obscure languages, Romanoff, increasingly enamored of everything the free world claimed to stand for, managed to find a sponsor in Boston (a Yiddish poet who had emigrated to the Jewish Autonomous Region of Birobidzhan in 1935 and, after failing to acclimate to the huge mosquitoes, returned home) and, as a Displaced Person, arrived in New York harbor in 1952. One year later, Stalin died and Romanoff was admitted to Harvard University as an undergraduate with a full scholarship. Six years later, in what all the tenured professors deemed an act of prodigious will, he deposited his voluminous dissertation—an elaborate treatise on the philosophy of Russian history—and received his Ph.D. as well as an immediate offer to stay and teach. Romanoff accepted and, in the early 1960s, just after having turned thirty, received tenure for the three books he had published—all massive tomes that advanced an excitingly new interpretation of the Russian state and nation. It was unclear which of his colleagues had actually pored over the trilogy, but all agreed that such extraordinary productivity had to be rewarded and that everything had to be done to keep their young Russian colleague tightly bound to the Harvard Common and its scarlet brick walls. Especially impressive was Romanoff's apparent command of some thirty languages, ranging from Latin to ancient Greek to Avar and Old Church Slavonic, and his self-taught ability to read ancient Norse runes. The young man was a genius, so much was clear, and his place was at the American Cambridge, so much was also clear.

Romanoff had no romantic liaisons during this time or, at least, none that people were aware of—and this despite his exerting a magnetic influence on Radcliffe's women professors and coeds, who were invariably enchanted by the tall, blond-haired, blue-eyed Russian who, unlike his colleagues in frumpy tweed jackets and stained knit ties, always wore three-piece suits, silk ties, and, most alluringly perhaps, French cuffs with silver cufflinks. A fedora, exactly the color of his suit, broad-rimmed, and always tilted, completed the irresistible picture.

According to one especially malicious rumor, possibly

spread by an envious colleague, Romanoff was a homosexual—he was too elegant not to be—and his unorthodox proclivities, which he supposedly pursued in the seediest side streets of Boston's Combat Zone, were the real reason for his decision to leave for the decadent West. Some of Romanoff's colleagues held their noses, others looked the other way. No one believed that particular quality—some called it a deficiency—merited expulsion or condemnation. Romanoff himself knew of the rumor and shrugged it off. First things first, he decided. First tenure and an academic career and then a wife and perhaps a family.

Meanwhile, his trilogy had received rave reviews in all the leading academic journals, in North America as well as Western Europe. It had been translated into German, French, and Italian and a Soviet publisher had even expressed interest in a Russian edition. Since Romanoff was technically a deserter—and Soviet deserters always got shot—some historians, mostly inveterate Cold Warriors with checkered backgrounds in Eastern Europe, wondered how and why his infraction could have been overlooked by the Kremlin, but, with Stalin quite dead and the Thaw in full swing, it made sense that the Soviet authorities might want to turn a new leaf and court the most prominent Russian historian in the West—all the more so as his views on Russian history coincided so closely with those of the Party.

Romanoff submitted that ancient Russia be reconceptualized as "Rasha," which he pronounced Rah-shah. He had dug deeply in the archives in Leningrad and Moscow—as well as in those in Berlin, Oslo, Stockholm, and Helsinki—and discovered remarkable documents that demonstrated beyond a reasonable doubt that a distinct Slavic civilization had existed in the geographic space between today's Leningrad and Moscow as early as the fifth century Anno Domini. That alone was cause for academic acclaim. But Romanoff also claimed to have shown that this civilization spoke a form of proto-Russian that shared some remarkable similarities with modern Russian. Moreover, these proto-Russian Slavs had attacked and conquered Scandinavia's Vikings in the seventh century, establishing a loosely held state-like polity that called itself Rasha.

These findings, all backed by serious research that resulted in the unexpected discovery of heretofore unknown documents, were sensational. They upended all existing theories of the formation of East Slavic civilization, placed Rasha—and, thus, Russia—squarely within these formative processes, and completely disproved the so-called Varangian Theory, according to which the Vikings had settled and gave political form to the Slavic lands in the ninth century.

Not surprisingly, Romanoff's work met with the enthusiastic approval of aging White Russian historians and pundits in North America and Europe. He was hailed as the new Kliuchevsky by some, as the new Solovyov by others, and as the new "tsar of Russian studies" by all. The Soviets responded with equal enthusiasm, delighted by Romanoff's demonstration that the ethnic roots of the Soviet Russian state reached back into antiquity, further even than their own propagandists posited. But the best part was, as far as the Soviets were concerned, that this theory implied that the "Rashan" people had to be as naturally supportive of proto-communism as they were naturally inclined to speak proto-Russian. Ukrainian, Polish, and other non-Russian historians were distressed by Romanoff's findings, claiming they reduced their national histories to appendages of Rasha's, while Germans, in both parts of the divided country, applauded Romanoff's efforts for the exact same reason. By cleansing Central and European history of the non-Russians, Romanoff had effectively given priority to two strands—one Rashan, one German—and thereby asserted the historical destiny and geopolitical primacy of both states, as well as both languages and nations, in the region. Remarkably, both the German left and right found Romanoff's arguments compelling, even if bits did not quite fit into their ideological worldviews.

His trilogy was followed by two more, each involving in-depth elaborations of his original theory and the meticulous use of archival sources. By the mid-sixties, Romanoff was in possession of the Pobedonostsev Chair of Russian Studies. His teaching load was reduced to one seminar per year on a topic of his choice. He was given an enormous, high-ceilinged office in one of the university's most august halls; two secretaries, Masha and Sasha, both Russian émigrés who, like Romanov, had spent several years in the Displaced Person camps in Germany, manned his IBM computers (he had three, while his colleagues had at most one), took care of his correspondence, which grew exponentially, and handled his schedule, which included meetings with world leaders, prominent foreign and domestic intellectuals, as well as journalists searching for a good story. There was even talk of a Nobel Prize, though no one could specify the field for which a historian would qualify. Needless to say, many of his colleagues, especially those who were most forthright in their laudations, envied him with a passion that bordered on obsession. Romanoff knew that his friends were mostly wolves in sheep's clothing, but, as with the rumors of his homosexuality, he adopted a pose of serene indifference and measured equanimity. Whether or not that pose corresponded to his internal feelings was another matter, but, as no mortal could divine them, the question was moot.

*

Romanoff's speech at the Free University on that Tuesday before all hell broke loose had gone well, as he knew it would. Addressing adulatory crowds—and the Germans were adulatory to an almost embarrassing degree—had become routine for Romanoff. Salutations followed by a joke or two, preferably with a heavy dose of self-irony related to his surname, followed by a superficial account of his latest findings followed by a summary of What It All Means always produced the desired effect, especially from audiences that could imagine no other response.

Preceded by obsequious bows to *Herr Doktor* or *Herr Doktor Professor*, the questions that came after he finished to resounding applause were all boilerplate, except for one, asked by a long-haired student in a wrinkled t-shirt and faded jeans who wanted to know Romanoff's stand on Baader, Meinhof, and their comrades in the Red Army Faction. Romanoff recognized the names, but knowing only that they were terrorists and that terrorism was a problem in West Germany, he elegantly sidestepped the query by stating that, given the nature of the event, he thought it proper to address strictly academic questions only. It was later in the day, as he bantered with the journalists who were supposed to interview him, that he learned that the Baader-Meinhof gang had just set off several bombs in protest against the American war in Vietnam and Germany's Nazi past. He shrugged, not from indifference but from ignorance. His seeming insouciance about an underground movement that hoped to destabilize Germany and introduce communism raised a few journalistic eyebrows, but Romanoff, perhaps truthfully, perhaps not, insisted that his scholarship forced him to live in the distant past and, thus, to treat the immediate present as most people treated the distant past. The interview, in any case, also went well.

Next day's story in one of Springer's least reputable newspapers was all the more shocking as it followed on the heels of two days of unqualified success. *"Russisches Monster!"* cried the front-page headline, in thick crimson type no less. *"Er hat uns vergewaltigt als unsere Heimat in Ruinen lag,"* ran the subheading: "He raped us as our homeland lay in ruins." The five women were identified only by letters. The story proceeded to describe, in lurid detail, just how the blond-haired "beast" with blue eyes and the "soul of Ivan the Terrible" had thrown himself on each of the five women and, with bayonet pressed against their throats, had torn at their clothes and "inserted his member" into the "hearts of their quivering womanhood." How can you be certain that your attacker was Professor Romanoff? the reporter had asked each of the women. All had responded identically: "His cold eyes and ironic sneer are unforgettable." Bollow ended her piece with a rhetorical question: "Dare the Russian monster who raped Germany as she lay defenseless go free?" As the letters to the editor that appeared in subsequent issues indicated, Berliners unanimously agreed that the answer was no.

Romanoff's West German colleagues recommended he ignore "that trash" and concentrate on the only thing that mattered—his academic work. "It's obvious nonsense," one of them summarized the consensus, "and the only way to deal with nonsense is to pretend it doesn't exist." Romanoff initially agreed, but then came the weekend edition of the Springer rag, which contained photographs of drunken Soviet soldiers below the heading: "*Warum schweigst du?*" The implication, however underhanded, was self-evident: that Romanoff had been in the Red Army was proof positive of his complicity in the crimes, while his continued silence was nothing less than a tacit admission of the veracity of the accusations.

A response of some kind was becoming unavoidable, so he agreed to a Sunday evening press conference in the offices of the *Berliner Zeitung*. The timing was bad, however, as most Germans, including the *BZ*'s own staffers, stayed home to watch Frankfurt play Munich and the only journalist who showed up was the aggressively inclined Bollow. She lit cigarette after cigarette, crossed and uncrossed her legs, and made no secret of her obvious impatience. Rather than engage her in a one-on-one confrontation that would enervate him and serve no purpose, the visibly disappointed Romanoff, who had been chain smoking at the podium, coughed politely and cancelled the event.

"What do you have to hide, *Herr Doktor*?" she cried as he left the room.

"*Nichts*," he said, flashing a disarming smile, "nothing at all."

Next day's headline in the Springer paper read, "*Niemand glaubt dem Monster von Berlin*," and went on to state that the absence of journalists at Romanoff's press conference proved that "no one believed the monster of Berlin." Bollow also reproduced her exchange with Romanoff, while conveniently eliding his pithy response to her provocative question.

Things were getting out of control, so Romanoff decided to confer with his colleagues and develop a strategy of counterattack. Adalbert Schmidt, a medieval historian who also lectured at Humboldt University in the other Berlin, suggested they take a closer look at "this Bollow *Weib*."

"Who is this woman?" Schmidt asked. "We know why Springer wants to disrupt your efforts at promoting a German-Russian reconciliation, but what's her game? And she has to have a game. Everyone has. This is Berlin, after all."

"Perhaps she was in the *Bund Deutscher Mädel*?" Rudolf Bethmann, a classicist who specialized in ancient Rome, opined in reference to the girls' version of the Hitler Youth. "Or perhaps her father was in the Party? Everyone's father was. That would do the trick."

"As was everyone's mother," Schmidt snickered.

After Romanoff asked whether "you gentlemen would mind doing some digging," they happily agreed to pursue whichever channels each had to determine just what this Bollow *Weib*'s angle was. Romanoff also proposed investigating the backgrounds of his five accusers; one of his *Berliner Zeitung* interviewers, Gisela Urban, agreed to devote some time to that.

"Don't think I'm doing this as a favor, *Herr Doktor*," she pointed out, lest Romanoff have any illusions about the degree of her commitment. "We have our ethical standards to protect. I'm doing this because it's an excellent story and the German people have a right to know."

Following their meeting with Romanoff, Schmidt and Bethmann retired to a bar and had a few beers and sausages. Both agreed that they had no intention of doing any digging. Romanoff was a star; they weren't. He wore snappy three-piece suits; they didn't. He was adored and feted; they weren't. He would survive a scandal; they wouldn't. His solicitude for them and their careers had always been nonexistent. Moreover, this affair was a no-win situation for Romanoff and anyone associated with him. Even if he was eventually vindicated—and neither was certain that the charges were easily refutable fabrications—his name would have been sullied. And the last thing either of them needed—especially since ancient and medieval studies subsisted on minimal budgets anyway—was to appear supportive of a man whose career could very well go up in flames. No, they winked at each other, the esteemed Professor Serge Romanoff of the esteemed Harvard University was on his own.

*

Bollow claimed to have tracked down the women after they had—independently of one another, they insisted—contacted the Springer newspaper on the day Romanoff's interview appeared in the *Berliner Zeitung*. That wasn't quite true. In reality, they knew one another from a left-leaning women's organization dedicated to cleaning the environment, banning nuclear weapons, promoting women's rights, and hastening Germany's departure from the North Atlantic Treaty Organization. The group, *Frauen für Frieden*, met once a week in the Kreuzberg district in a building inhabited by a motley collection of non-dogmatic Marxists, Leninists, Stalinists, Gramsciites, and Maoists committed to striking capitalism's death knell as well as a handful of indifferent anarchists who spent much of their days panhandling and reading Bakunin and Kropotkin.

The process by means of which the women became acquainted was gradual. Two of them, referred to as K and O in Bollow's account, realized they had more than politics in common during an FfF role-playing exercise that, while intended to increase their empathy for the quotidian hardships of the Soviet people, unintentionally opened their eyes to their shared experience of rape. The other three, referred to as L, M, and N by Bollow, joined K and O in a subcommittee devoted to women's rights. It was during one of their deliberations, as they were sharing personal stories of discrimination, that they learned that they had all been sexually abused in mid-May of 1945. They didn't know the perpetrator happened to be the same Russian soldier until the Romanoff interview appeared and it dawned upon them that the man in the photographs was an older version of the youth who had violated them.

Bollow, whom they contacted after being snubbed by several left-wing papers, expressed reservations about their story.

Were they sure? Absolutely, they replied. How could they be sure after thirty years? One doesn't forget the face of the monster that raped you, K replied. Aren't they afraid an innocent man's reputation might be ruined? He was guilty, M and N asserted. Wasn't it possible that their memories were faulty and that one woman's story had influenced the others? Out of the question! O cried. Are you impugning women's capacity to remember facts and think rationally? Very well, Bollow decided, I'll do the story, but only if my editor approves it. He did, as she knew he would. There was no resisting a piece that demonized the Soviets for crimes against humanity, while also depicting Germans as victims, and not just as perpetrators. Heino Funcke, the editor, also knew the article would make the far left, especially the terrorists grouped around the Baader-Meinhof gang, squirm. That alone was worth the price of admission.

Although she didn't express her doubts openly, Bollow felt uneasy about the article. On the one hand, like Funcke, she believed it would have enormous political resonance and strike a body blow to the left. That was good. On the other hand, the women's story would have been more persuasive had they not been friends and colleagues in some crackpot organization dedicated to something as unimaginative as peace. She doubted they would have resorted to intentional mendacity or manipulation —although one never knew with these crazy left-wing groups that occupied Berlin's run-down housing and hoped to put an end to war with ungrammatical leaflets and tree hugging. But she was concerned about the appearance, if not reality, of collusion. The professor, being an effete elitist from Harvard, was probably a *Schweinhund*, but, if the women's story cracked, for whatever reason and even if only a bit, they would be discredited, he vindicated, and she pilloried.

On the other hand, there was the political import of the women's revelations to consider. The Bavarians would be delighted by any slander of the Russians. As would the Christian Democrats. The Socialists and Communists would be up in arms and claim that the newspaper had launched a despicable campaign of unvarnished lies. West Germany's predominantly left-leaning intellectuals, spearheaded by incomprehensible philosophers like Jürgen Habermas, would deny the very possibility of the women's story being true. Bollow knew the argument. Germany and the Germans had started the war. They had destroyed millions of people, including six million Jews. They had no one to blame for the destruction of their country and its people but themselves. To focus on the mass rapes committed by the Russians was, in effect, to imply that they, and not the Germans, were the war criminals.

Everyone knew about the militarily superfluous carpet bombing of Hamburg and Dresden that had killed hundreds of thousands of civilians. But no one dared speak of it. And no one dared speak of it in the same breath as one spoke of German crimes. That was *Relativierung*—or presenting German atrocities as only relatively worse than, or relatively the same as, Allied atrocities. Indeed, there could be no such thing as Allied atrocities. Those were the preserve of the Germans and only of the Germans. Violating this unwritten code elicited merciless criticism in the past. In today's disjointed world, with the Baader-Meinhof people running amok amid a clueless police and a confused populace, violating it could result in violent reprisals, even death—and that struck Bollow as a decidedly unattractive option.

It was 1975 and both Andreas Baader and Ulrike Meinhof were in Stammheim prison. Although they had been captured in 1972, the Red Army Faction was alive and well in the underground, presumably planning new strikes against American imperialism and German fascism. The government had adopted an Anti-Radical Decree that included a ban on Communists' teaching in Germany's public schools. The left had squealed with outrage, but the threat posed by Baader, Meinhof, and their followers was real. Bollow recognized that German democracy was flawed. The country's attitude toward Nazi war criminals had been, and still was, too lax. And the middle class was too stuffy even for her post-radical tastes. But the terrorists were no alternative. They offered only violence and the prospect of a revolution that, if successful, would transform West Germany into East Germany. One didn't have to be a Springer supporter to have serious doubts about the appeal of Soviet-style communism. The Wall dividing Berlin was sufficient proof of the unattractiveness of the East's political and economic system. If communism was, as its propagandists insisted, paradise, then why keep people out and why would anyone inside want to leave?

It was quite simple, really. The Baader-Meinhof terrorists had to be crushed, even if that meant employing methods that bordered on the extreme. Democracy had a right to defend itself. If it failed to do so, as it did in 1933, wouldn't the barbarians come to power once again? The left, according to Bollow, saw a threat only on the right, but a bit of perspicacity and some knowledge of world history doubtless sufficed to persuade any reasonable person that the left generated as many threats, if not more, to humanity as the right. How many millions did Stalin kill? Or Lenin before him? Or their apostles in China, Cuba, and Vietnam? What an irony that the Baader-Meinhof gang should call itself a faction of, of all things, the Red Army! Its hordes drove back the Wehrmacht—and the sacrifices the Russians and their non-Russian henchmen made were an eternal tribute to their bravery—but they also drove out millions of German civilians from their ancestral homes in Poland, Czechoslovakia, and the Baltic states and unleashed a reign of terror on German womanhood in 1945.

Why commit the mass rapes? Why assault several million defenseless women and pubescent girls—as well as not a few grandmothers? Hadn't the Russian brutes already amply demonstrated their exceptional courage to the world, the Germans, and themselves? Hadn't they achieved victory completely and absolutely by the time the rapes began in earnest? Fair enough, their hatred of the Germans—of all Germans, regardless of age or sex—was deep and understandable. So, why not shoot the women instead? Why spread their thighs and insert their hungry *Schwänze* into their unwilling—she recalled the ugly Russian word—*pizdy*? This wasn't hate. This was a desire to humiliate, to demonstrate to the women, and ultimately to their men—their husbands, fathers, brothers, and sons—that they had become utterly powerless, that the brutes were now in charge—so much so that they could commit unspeakable crimes with unrestrained abandon, in the full knowledge that nothing, absolutely nothing, would happen to them as a result. This was the jungle and the Russians were its kings.

Bollow couldn't restrain a smirk as she considered that the German armed forces—and especially the murderous SS and SD, the *Sicherheitsdienst*—had introduced the jungle to Ukraine, Belorussia, and Russia in 1941. We had been the beasts then; now it was the turn of the Russians. Was it any consolation that our blond-haired, blue-eyed soldiers hadn't engaged in mass rapes? No, she concluded bitterly, they had merely burned and shot and gassed and cremated, sometimes while reading Goethe or listening to Beethoven. So, who was the greater beast? The question couldn't be answered, and definitely not in the facile manner of the left. Crimes were crimes. If those of the Nazis were worthy of condemnation, then so, too, were those of the Russians.

These considerations made it all the more imperative for the women's account to be air-tight. Much more was at stake here than five victims of abuse. The questions they raised were precisely those that everyone ignored. Was it possible to treat some or all Germans as victims? Was it possible for the Allies in general and the Russians in particular to have committed crimes and, thus, to be criminals? And how would the answers to both questions affect how Germans, Americans, and the so-called West viewed humanity's propensity for violence? So much of German political culture regarded Germany as exceptional, but what if it was the norm? Bollow shuddered at her ruminations and their implications. If Hitler was immanent in all mankind, then Baader and Meinhof were our collective future. Did the five women even begin to imagine the size of the Pandora's Box they had opened?

*

Romanoff denied the accusations unhesitatingly and, after his initial irascible reaction, refrained from counter-accusations of intentional slander, insisting instead that the five women must have misremembered. Wartime was intrinsically confusing. When bombs exploded and guns were fired, when rubble bounced and walls came crashing down, when thousands of soldiers, all hungry, tired, desperate, and angry, moved back and forth and back and forth across some terrain for days on end, it was perfectly natural for survivors of such storms to mistake confusion for reality. Were the women raped? There was no doubt that they were. Was he the rapist? Of course not. Back in 1945, he had been a confused young boy of fifteen, barely capable of carrying his knapsack and rifle, terrified of being shot by some diehard Nazi fanatic, and completely indifferent to the opposite sex. He had lost some twenty kilograms since enlisting and couldn't have forced himself on anybody, even if he had tried. Naturally, he sympathized with his accusers. Having experienced Nazi violence, he empathized with their encounter with Russian violence. He'd even be happy to meet with them and set the story straight. But did he do it? No, he told whichever journalist was willing to meet with him, no, no, and yet again no!

The Soviet historians who attended the conference displayed extraordinary initiative and quickly generated a petition, signed by several dozen Russian, Polish, Czech, Ukrainian, and Belorussian scholars, in which they insisted that a scholar of Romanoff's genius could not possibly have such a blemish on his past. It was *unglaublich*—unthinkable! Romanoff, they wrote, had produced several pathbreaking trilogies on the origins of the Russian state and nation. He had won prizes and received accolades; he had reached the pinnacle of his profession while remaining a decent, honest, and trustworthy colleague who respected all the men and women with whom he came into contact. It was slander to suggest that *Herr Doktor Professor* Romanoff could be anything but a paragon of virtue, a seeker of truth, a devotee of Clio—and an avid supporter of peaceful coexistence, proletarian internationalism, and the friendship of peoples. The signatories stopped just short of declaring Romanoff a card-carrying Marxist.

Not unexpectedly, neither Romanoff's denials nor the petition did much to stop the flow of articles. Several days after the initial accusations appeared, the Springer newspaper ran profiles and photographs of each of the women (with faces blotted out, an effect that enhanced the aura of evil), under the general heading, *"Ich habe überlebt! Die deutsche Frau ist unbesiegbar"* (I survived! The German woman is invincible). The profiles were vague. All the women had had happy childhoods. All had hated Hitler, even as they feared to express that hatred in direct action. All had bemoaned the fate of the Jews. All had managed to scrimp and save and eke out an existence in the hungry postwar years. All had eventually married or remarried (two had lost husbands on the front) and come to live normal, ordinary, decent lives. All had also believed that their trauma would remain buried. But seeing his photograph in the *Berliner Zeitung* led to a sudden rush of painful memories and the realization that their awful past had appeared, almost like a malignant spirit, in the form of a Harvard historian. Even they had difficulty believing that this distinguished academic, who clearly preferred dusty archives to living people, could have been their tormentor in 1945. But, alas, he was—and it was their duty, to themselves, to their children, and to Germany, to speak the truth, no matter the consequences. Scores of sympathetic letters to the editor poured in. Most condemned Romanoff and defended the women. A few proffered that he be dispatched on the first train to Auschwitz. Those Funcke dispatched to the trash bin.

Worse, and adding proverbial fuel to the fire, a variety of other German newspapers had picked up the story. Radio Liberty, Radio Free Europe, Deutsche Welle, and the BBC also reported on the ongoing controversy, thereby ensuring that

Romanoff's difficulties would become well known to their audiences in the Communist bloc. His many Russian friends within Soviet universities, research institutions, and the media could be counted on to regard the scandal with a huge lump of salt, as just another underhanded attempt by the Western intelligence services to disrupt détente by discrediting Russian scholarship and culture. Romanoff also knew that many of these friends were decidedly of the fair-weather variety and that, given the opportunity, would gladly grab any sharp implement and stab him in the back. Sooner or later, *The New York Times*, the London *Times*, *Le Monde*, and other serious western papers would join the fray. There was little to be done to stop their commentary or reportage, but it might be possible to change the story by offering an exclusive interview. What had he to lose? She'd be aggressive and insulting, but he'd remain calm and rational and present his side of the story as objectively as possible. What had he to lose? Nothing. Besides, by drawing her into a conversation, he'd have the chance to establish emotional bonds and thaw her cold demeanor.

Not accidently perhaps, the Soviet diplomats in Berlin had come to similar conclusions. Officially, the case had nothing to do with the Soviet Union. After all, though once a Red Army soldier, Romanoff was now a citizen in good standing of the United States. But there were two points that did concern the propagandists in the Communist Party and the secret police, the KGB. Accusations against Romanoff the ex-soldier concerned the Red Army in its entirety. He was not just a metonym for the Soviet armed forces that liberated Berlin; the rapes he had supposedly committed were an infinitesimally small portion of the total number of rapes allegedly committed by the heroic Red Army. If the case against Romanoff went badly, then there was no way for the army to be spared similar calumnies. The Soviets could always count on their friends, sympathizers, and fellow travelers in Germany for support, but the embarrassment could be significant, especially as the accusations were launched during the thirtieth anniversary of the end of the war.

The other point concerned Romanoff's scholarship. His claim that Rasha had already existed in the fifth century was a boon to Soviet propaganda, which labored intensively to demonstrate that the "leading role" of the Russian people within the Soviet Union was a natural outgrowth of their leading role in the historical formation of Eastern Europe. If Russia could trace its roots to Rasha, and if Rasha predated the Vikings and, perhaps, even the Avars, Huns, and other barbarians, then the case for Russian primacy would be indisputable.

Moreover, if, as Romanoff argued, the ancient Rashans had already spoken an early variant of what was eventually to become modern Russian, then the case for the primacy of the Russian language—for its indispensability and inevitability as the primary means of "inter-nationality communication"—was equally unassailable. Naturally, there would be elements within the Soviet Union, primarily retrograde Ukrainian, Lithuanian, Estonian, and Latvian "bourgeois nationalists," who would dispute the indisputable, citing their own sources and making their own claims for national authenticity. They could be dealt with easily enough—by means of prolonged visitations to labor colonies in the Siberian forests. What mattered most was that their ideas would be given new life if Romanoff's research were put in doubt by virtue of his past peccadilloes. And, as the ideological experts in the Party and secret police knew, it was erroneous ideas, and not people, that constituted the greatest obstacle to the full-scale victory of Soviet communism.

Within a few days of the scandal's eruption on that fateful Thursday, what began as a simple accusation directed against a prominent professor had grown into an issue—or *Fall*, as the Germans put it—that affected the interests of several constituencies. Intellectuals and professors felt threatened by the accusations. The German right saw in them an opportunity to score points against the left. The German left viewed the accusations as undermining the capitalist critique in general and the Red Army Faction in particular. Sieglinde Bollow realized that her career, and reputation, were on the line. The five women desired vindication for the unspeakable traumas they had experienced. And Professor Romanoff wanted his name to be cleared for perfectly understandable reasons. The stage was set for an intensification of the clash.

But, before that clash could occur, three incendiary bombs went off in department stores in Berlin, Frankfurt, and Dortmund. The RAF took credit for the explosions and released a statement saying that its war against imperialism and capitalism would continue until Germany became a socialist state. Fortunately, there were no deaths and the damage was minimal, implying that the moderates in the movement still retained the upper hand. The government declared it would do everything necessary to protect the *Rechtsstaat*—the rule of law state—and democracy from the cowardly terrorists who resorted to stealth because they lacked the people's support. *"Das Volk ist mit uns,"* claimed the Chancellor, his hand pounding the podium, at a televised press conference. "The people are with us." That could have very well been the case, but, even so, people's nerves were noticeably on edge, contributing to a climate of fear that only aggravated Romanoff's position. Now that everyone could be a potential terrorist, it almost followed that everyone—even an American professor who wrote about recondite historical events —could be a rapist.

CHAPTER TWO

The women, though identified as K, L, M, N, and O by Sieglinde Bollow, were fully real, living human beings. K was Ursula Lange, forty years old; L was Liselotte Goebbels, forty-three; M was Maria Wurlitzer, fifty. N, Johanna Habermann, and O, Heidi Hardt, were twins in their late sixties, possibly in their early seventies, who had lost their documents during the war and were somewhat hard of hearing, though still fully in possession of their wits. If their stories were to be believed, Lange was raped at the age of ten, Goebbels at thirteen, Wurlitzer at twenty, and Habermann and Hardt at about forty. The ages of Lange and Goebbels made even skeptics wince. They had been children at the time of the alleged outrages. Even if Romanoff was innocent of the charges, it seemed indisputable that some other Russian had violated them—which meant that Russian soldiers indiscriminately attacked children as well as adult women. The latter might be deemed responsible for Hitler's outrages, but the former?

The question was rhetorical for most Germans, but not for all. Barbara Eichendorf, who moonlighted for the Soviets as, among other things, a translator, and her left-wing comrades saw in Lange and the fortuitously named Goebbels a rare opportunity to drive home their argument that *all* Germans were not just responsible in some vaguely moralistic way for the war and the gas chambers; no, they were actually guilty, no less guilty than the reprehensible men who had been sentenced to death at Nuremberg and only slightly less guilty than the instigator of the madness, Hitler himself. The culture, the mentality, the spirit or what Germans called the *Geist*, and the history of this accursed *Volk* had to be eradicated in a swift act of violence and a completely new nation, one committed to peace and socialism, should replace it. Evolution, of the kind practiced by the criminal Christian Democrats Konrad Adenauer, Ludwig Erhard, and Kurt Kiesinger as well as by the no less collaborationist Socialists-who-were-no-socialists, Willy Brandt and Helmut Schmidt, was an obvious and manifest failure. It led only to the consolidation of the Nazis' hold on the institutions of society and state; it would lead, inexorably and inevitably, to the revival of Nazism, the reemergence of a second Hitler, and a third world war of even greater proportions than the first two.

On these points of doctrine, Eichendorf and her comrades agreed fully with Meinhof and Ensslin. Eichendorf also supported the Red Army Faction's determination to fight imperialism with the only means the imperialists understood—violence. You steal from the world; we will steal from you. You slay Vietnamese babies; we will kill fascist soldiers. You cherish capitalism, we will destroy it. But Meinhof and Ensslin also appeared to believe that the Germans could be transformed and the world thereby saved. They were wrong. The nation had to be uprooted—physically if necessary, culturally if possible. And that meant that all Germans, young and old, men and women, were equally guilty. All had to pay. And all would, especially if this opportunity to highlight German children's complicity in crimes against humanity were to be exploited to maximum political and ideological advantage. Ironically, it was Baader and his crude combination of thuggery and anarchism who most closely resonated with Eichendorf and her group. The handsome hooligan only had a vague understanding of why he had joined the movement, but his instincts—that everything had to be smashed—were on target, even if ideologically incoherent. Eichendorf's group called itself the Revolutionary Red Army Faction and its violence would be directed, not at department stores and individual representatives of German capitalism and fascism, but at the ordinary Germans who made Hitler, followed him, and revered him. Thanks to Eichendorf's mastery of Latin in middle school, the RRAF's slogan was a variant of Cato's "Carthage must be destroyed": "*Germania delenda est.*"

Eichendorf's no-holds-barred commitment to a pure revolutionary spirit that would rain fire on the Sodom and Gomorrah that was West Germany and her unconditional faith in a socialist millenarianism may have been the product of her upbringing. Her parents, both high-ranking Nazis, had been executed for war crimes just after her birth, when de-Nazification was still the fashion in post-war Germany. Her foster parents, a tight-lipped Protestant minister in Bremen and his thin wife, never failed to remind Barbara of her sinful genesis—and of the sinful origins of all mankind. "Repeat after me," he would say before every meal: "*Im Menschen sitzt der Teufel und der muss ausgerottet werden.*" "Yes," she would answer timorously, "in every person sits the devil who must be exterminated." One of Barbara's friends, upon learning of her foster-father's severe views, once remarked that Barbara's own inclination to divide the world into the damned and the saved now made perfect sense. Barbara slapped her face, cursed her impudence, and ended the relationship. In time, her magnetic personality—some comrades even spoke of her charisma—and unalterable convictions attracted a small coterie of radical followers who desired revolution but believed the RAF had sold out.

The five women were oblivious of such ideological nuances. They had suffered humiliation and, having identified the perpetrator as Professor Romanoff, were determined to seek justice and, possibly, a bit of revenge as well. Their recent sympathies were on the left, but theirs was a well-meaning, warmhearted left-wing activism that centered on the importance of preserving the world's environment and including in that enterprise as many people, as many voices and perspectives, as possible. They knew of the Red Army Faction and its imprisoned leaders—what German did not?—but had little sympathy for their tactics and no understanding of their ideology and strategy—all the more so since, at heart, they remained German *Frauen*, and not *Revoluzzer*. And as German women, they were, first and foremost, German—which, as both Bollow and

Eichendorf realized, meant that they were products of twentieth-century Germany and all its complexes, phobias, madnesses, and idiocies. And that, in turn, meant that they were all defined by the Nazi past, a past that, at first glance, seemed to be utterly foreign to their lives and to their involvement in *Frauen für Frieden*, but which had molded them, their men, as well as the entire post-war German past, present, and future.

*

In mid-1945, Ursula Lange (K) had been a ten-year old school girl who, like most of her friends, did well in German history and literature and poorly in mathematics and science. Her teachers described her as patient, studious, and hard-working. She excelled in sports, especially in track and field, and enjoyed hiking in the forests outside Berlin and swimming in the Krumme Lanke with the other girls from the *Bund Deutscher Mädel*. The small peanut-shaped lake, surrounded by ominously opaque trees and offering little space for frivolous sunbathing, inspired Ursula to let fly her imagination and, as she swam out to the middle and looked around, she could see Teutonic tribes honing their axes in preparation for the decisive battle with the Roman interlopers.

Ursula particularly loved wearing the Bund's uniform, which her mother always kept crisply ironed, and marching in parades, banners flapping, feet moving in unison, steely faces fixed on the future. Needless to say, she adored the Führer. He was wise, he loved his people, and he had dedicated his life to making Germany a prosperous state. And, as everyone knew, he loved children. He also defended Germany against its many enemies, who envied German success at building a strong country and were determined to destroy the German people. Our brave soldiers suffered immensely on behalf of their *Volk* in Russia, Africa, Italy, and France. But their noble sacrifices would eventually contribute to building an even stronger Germany. The Führer would see to that. But first the war had to be won and everyone, from the smallest child to the oldest grandfather or grandmother, had to contribute. Ursula did—by collecting scrap metal and plastic and, most important, by maintaining morale and keeping a lookout for enemies of the Führer and enemies of the people who, incomprehensibly, hated Germany and its leader.

Ursula drew special pride from having uncovered—and denounced—one of her classmates, a certain Greta Schabowski, for having drawn the Führer's distinctive mustache on a picture of the devil and giggled while showing it to her friends. Aghast at the sacrilege, Ursula had run to the teacher and told her of Greta's treasonous behavior. Greta was punished accordingly and her parents were summoned to the local Gestapo headquarters for a lesson on child rearing. In turn, Ursula received a special commendation and was lauded by all the teachers. Her parents beamed with pride, but only outwardly. Their two sons, Fritz and Hans, had had their young throats cut by partisans in the Belorussian swamps during the "strategic retreat" that followed the "temporary setback" at Stalingrad; thereafter, both mother and father came to experience a few pangs of doubt about the winnability of the war. They never conveyed their views to the child, keeping them within the confines of their bedroom, where they hid beneath a ratty down comforter and exchanged hushed whispers. Once, after returning to bed from the toilet, Ursula overheard the whispering and wondered why the virus of secrecy had also infected *Vati* and *Mutti*.

Ursula's father, Albert, a minor bureaucrat in the waterworks department of Berlin, had joined the Party after the Reichstag fire in 1933, when he realized that the winds had shifted and that membership in the ruling elite was now imperative. Ursula's mother, Andrea, was a librarian who, unlike most Germans, actually read all of *Mein Kampf*, as well as the works of Alfred Rosenberg, Georg Strasser, and other Nazi thinkers, and, while not fully persuaded by their self-declared genius, eventually stumbled upon the conclusion that their ideas, though not quite on the level of Hegel, Kant, and Schopenhauer, just might revitalize the spiritually spent German soul and raise the nation from the ranks of the near-dead. Eventually, she joined the *Na-*

tional Socialist Frauenschaft women's organization.

By 1944, both Albert and Andrea mostly feigned enthusiasm for the war, suspecting that the Führer had committed folly by attacking the Soviet Union and engaging in a two-front conflict. Was not the Führer repeating Napoleon's mistake? Did not the wise Bismarck do everything humanly possible to avoid just such an eventuality? mused Andrea. Neither she nor her husband had been to the USSR, but they knew that the country was vast, that its resources and population were huge, and that its leadership was ruthless as well as utterly indifferent to the well-being of its people. Stalin had no qualms about pursuing a scorched-earth policy and sacrificing ten Russians or twenty Ukrainians for every German. There were also rumors of dreadful camps for Jews and Gypsies and Slavs, but one couldn't be sure they weren't concocted by enemy propaganda. Could the nation of such Enlightenment thinkers as Goethe and Schiller —whom Andrea the librarian had read and admired—stoop so low? It seemed hardly likely.

In the second half of 1944 and the first half of 1945 the bombs fell with regular monotony on the Reich's capital and whatever residual enthusiasm for and belief in the regime that Albert and Andrea still possessed rapidly vanished. The news from the fronts was all bad, despite Goebbels's efforts to prettify it, and the daily bombardments, the collapsing roofs and walls, the smoke and stench of burning flesh, the crackle of broken glass underfoot were all reminders that the Führer's great project was on the verge of destruction. Had they been younger, had they no child, they might have fled or joined the resistance —or so they told themselves under the covers. But there was Ursula, the committed little Nazi, to take care of. And where was the resistance? How did one resist an all-powerful totalitarian regime that controlled everything outside one's bedroom? The answer was obvious. One did not, because one could not. They occasionally listened to BBC broadcasts breathlessly encouraging Germans to rise up against the oppressive Nazi system. Rise up, indeed! It was all too easy for German émigrés in London to dream of resistance and imagine themselves fighting the Nazi machine with a Luger in one hand and a copy of Kant's *Perpetual Peace* in the other. They should try to resist *here*—inside the *Vaterland*. Then they'd see that it was tantamount to suicide for yourself and murder for your family and friends.

There was nothing to be done, but to wait for the war to end and then, with a little luck, to survive Armageddon and the subsequent occupation. One could only hope that the liberators would be Americans or British, and not the hated Russians. Nazi propaganda had not been without effect and most Germans imagined the Slavs—and the *Russen* above all—as distended beasts with hairy faces, sharp teeth, cracked fingernails, and dull, bloodshot eyes. Since the Lange family happened to live in the eastern part of the city, it was the Red Army that drove out the remnants of the Wehrmacht and took control of their neighborhood. Like rats, the people hid in their homes or in cellars, fearful of the Russian hordes and the vengeance they would take.

Refugees from the east had brought accounts of terrifying Russian atrocities. Not even babies were spared. As for the women, they had all been raped—repeatedly, violently, and without exception. Ursula's mother resolved to sacrifice herself for her daughter. The soldiers would surely prefer a not unattractive woman of thirty to a ten-year old. For several days the strategy worked. Andrea offered herself to the Russians as they climbed the stairs to their home, their heavy boots thumping like a herd of wild elephants, with the result that she was raped —in point of fact, gang-raped—close to ten times in the course of a week. She never screamed and she never resisted, knowing that she was saving her daughter from the same fate. Her husband, on the other hand, felt an overwhelming sense of impotence, rage, and frustration. After the first rape, he hid in their apartment, beat his chest repeatedly and cried, and then became morose, withdrawn, and passive.

The rape of their daughter took place seven days after the occupation had set in, when the restless child resolved to violate her parents' order not to leave the apartment and, as they were busy in the kitchen trying to make a thin soup from the rotten beets and bones they had managed to find on the black market, descended the lightless staircase to the eerily quiet street outside. What Ursula saw shocked her. Everywhere were ruins. The army was nowhere to be seen. Red flags or red rags hung from windows. The swastikas were gone. The world she had known and loved and expected to last a thousand years had come to an end. Where was the Führer? Where were his trusted lieutenants, Goebbels and Himmler? Where were the brave soldiers of the Wehrmacht? Oh, how handsome, how invincible they had looked in their crisp uniforms and shiny boots as they marched off to victory!

She decided to explore some of the neighboring blocks and found the same. Could the wispy, unshaven shadows of men who picked at the refuse have once been Aryan warriors? As she stood amid the rubble and bent over to pick up a doll, someone shoved her, she fell to the ground with a cry, and then, before she could get to her feet, a Russian boy, blond-haired and blue-eyed, the perfect Aryan, but with bad breath, lay atop her and was spreading her virgin thighs. Ursula waited for the shadowy men, the defenders of German womanhood, to intervene, to save her, but they had all run—not for help, but to save themselves. That night, after she returned home bloodied and bruised and was washed, fed thin soup, and placed in bed, her father jumped out the window.

*

Liselotte Goebbels (L)—or Lotte as she was known to her friends—was thirteen in mid-1945. One sister had died in childbirth; another was in her twenties and worked in a factory producing ammunition for the front. Three brothers served in the army. One had the bad luck to have stumbled under a moving German tank during the rout of France in 1940. Another had joined Rommel's Afrika Korps, lost a leg near Khartoum, and now sold newspapers in a kiosk on Alexanderplatz. A third operated a flak gun somewhere in Austria, possibly in Vienna, possibly farther to the west. Lotte herself attended a girls' Gymnasium, where she excelled in Latin and Greek. A tall, lanky girl with the obligatory blonde hair and braids, she served, though perfunctorily, in the *Bund Deutscher Mädel*. It wasn't the incomprehensible ideology that distressed her. It was easy enough to ignore or, if need be, memorize. No, it was the forced gaiety, so similar to the ubiquitous *Kraft durch Freude* slogans and tours organized by her father. Who could oppose Strength through Joy? Who could object to weekend trips for German workers? Who wouldn't want to go on a cruise along Norway's fjords? There was no need to insist that we be joyful and gay. It was all quite simple. All we had to do was to look to the Führer for inspiration and *Kraft und Freude* would ineluctably follow.

She still recalled the day a lengthy motorcade with Hitler drove slowly past her school. The Führer stood in his coal-black cabriolet, his back straight, his belt buckle and buttons gleaming in the sunlight, his right hand raised, a benign, if slightly bemused smile on his lips—as if he couldn't quite understand what the commotion was all about. His car had stopped briefly in front of the school and a delegation of three excited girls, including Lotte, had given him a bouquet of freshly cut red roses, a symbol of their love of the man, the people, and the Reich. Lotte had carried the flowers and, as she handed them tremulously to Hitler, his right hand brushed against hers and then, wonder of wonders, he extended his left hand and stroked her head. Her entire body quivered and she realized just how the blind and lame must have felt when Christ had touched and healed them. Seeing her heightened emotional state, the good Führer had patted her ruddy cheek, saying *"Gutes Mäderl, gutes Mäderl."* A good girl, she had thought, I am and shall always be the Führer's good girl. As the motorcade resumed its course and the figure of the Führer disappeared behind a turn in the street, the feeling of loss so overwhelmed her that Lotte burst into tears, as did, almost on cue, her two friends. Their teachers consoled them and their fellow classmates envied them.

Joseph Goebbels, the Führer's propaganda mastermind,

was a very distant relative, a third or fourth cousin of her father, Detlev, and that connection accounted for his having landed the position of managing director of the *Kraft durch Freude* office in Wedding, a working-class district in Berlin's northeast. *Vati* used to speak of Joseph with great pride, but that was in the thirties and only in the first few years of the war. After Stalingrad, when the limbless and eyeless soldiers began returning *en masse* from the front and Cousin Joseph continued to insist that victory was still within easy reach, that all that it required was a concentration of the people's will and the continued brilliant leadership of the Führer, her father's invocations of him became less and less frequent. Few workers dared expressed their views openly, but it was a well-known fact that they rolled their eyes and made obscene gestures whenever the diminutive man began one of his infamous radio tirades.

Vati had been a member of the SA, the Storm Troopers, since 1928 or 1929, when the Depression hit Germany with great force and he had joined the vast and growing army of the unemployed. The SA *Kameraden* gave him a brown uniform, shiny black boots, a cudgel, a sense of purpose, and a living wage. In return, he would join them in frequent drinking bouts and the occasional street fights with Communists and *Aktionen* against Jews, anything from throwing bricks at storefront windows to kicking corpulent businessmen in their big fat Jewish asses. He even befriended Horst Wessel, the brave Storm Trooper martyred in some altercation with the rabid Reds. Horst later became the subject of an adulatory song and, when doing household chores, Lotte's father would sing its inspirational words:

> *The flag raised high! Our ranks closed tight!*
> *The SA marches with calm, steady step.*
> *The comrades shot dead by the Red Front and reaction*
> *March in spirit within our ranks.*

Detlev's wife, Gabriela, or Gabi, wasn't too happy with his SA antics, insisting that sooner or later they'd get him into trouble. Her nagging finally paid off in 1934. Detlev quietly exited the organization a few months before the Night of Long Knives, when Hitler arrested or executed his erstwhile SA comrades for threatening his hold on power. Detlev's departure couldn't have been better timed, with the result that what in retrospect came to be known as his "principled opposition" to the degenerate SA leader, Ernst Röhm, a crude man who liked boys, was eventually rewarded with a well-paying job with *Kraft durch Freude*. The position offered little excitement to a young man weaned on the Storm Troopers, but it offered him a refuge from the turbulence outside and enabled him to reach a *modus vivendi* with the new regime. Naturally, he joined the Party soon after he left the SA.

Gabi was delighted that her husband was no longer breaking heads and windows and devoted herself fulltime to her duties as mother and housewife. With Detlev occupying a high-profile job in the movement, Gabi had to insinuate herself into the *National Socialist-Frauenschaft*, where she became active in the local chapter's executive committee. The meetings bored her, as did the endless discussions of Nazi policy and Hitler's love of youth, but there was no alternative to feigning interest. The other women were usually too reticent to speak, so she resolved to make at least one comment, however anodyne, and ask one question, however naïve, at each meeting.

Apparently, her dissimulation was sufficiently persuasive to lead to a clandestine meeting, not on her initiative of course, with an agent of the Gestapo, a severe woman with her metallic hair tied in a tight bun, who gently asked if she might be willing to serve the Führer by keeping an eye on her colleagues and reporting back if she witnessed behavior or heard opinions unbecoming of a good German woman. Gabi couldn't refuse, so much was obvious even to her, so sometime in 1935 or 1936 she became an official informer for the secret police. Unnecessarily, the agent reminded her that Detlev and the children were not to be told about her service to the Party, Leader, and state. She didn't like keeping her husband in the dark about anything, but one had to make moral compromises for the good of the cause. At the same time, she noticed that her clandestine activity appeared to have produced some not unpleasant side benefits. Shopping became easier, the local tavern keeper began offering her and her husband free beers, her colleagues in the women's association treated her with greater respect, the butcher always gave her the best cut of meat at a discount. People had somehow discovered her new status or been told, discreetly to be sure, about it. Or, perhaps, they too were informers? In any case, Gabi soon became inured to her work and came to take its perks for granted.

Until the Allied bombing began in earnest, there was little to report on—much to the dissatisfaction of the stern woman with the bun. By mid- to late 1944, however, as the grumbling began and the carping became less indirect, her reports, which she wrote with growing reluctance and some shame, acquired greater substance. Some of the women were interrogated and returned to work with visibly bruised arms and black eyes. They blamed their injuries on their husbands, who appear to have all developed a sudden penchant for excessive drink, but Gabi knew better. One woman failed to return entirely and rumor had it that she and her family had moved to Munich, where her husband had been transferred. Or was it to Dachau?

Gabi's daughter, Lotte, ignored the rattling china and cracked walls and retained her wondrous fascination with the Führer—that memorable day remained firmly implanted in her memory—and kept a scrapbook of his photos that she cut out of magazines and newspapers. The great man appeared either deeply concerned—for the well-being of the nation, no doubt— or relaxed—usually with his dog or his friends—in all of them. A large portrait of Hitler hung above her bed, just below the cross. The Führer had a good face, a kind face, the face of a favorite uncle or grandfather. I shall, she decided, always love and honor and obey him, come what may. I shall always be his *"gutes Mäderl."*

Lotte's feelings about the Führer remained unchanged even after she was gang raped by some five to ten dirty, smelly, repulsive Russians. They all looked and barked alike, except for the tall blond-haired boy, whose features were distinctly German. As she rearranged her underclothes afterwards, she knew that the Führer had been right to call these dogs *Untermenschen*. The world would have been a far better place without them and with us, the *Übermenschen*, guiding human affairs for the benefit of the German *Volk*, the Aryan race, and all civilized peoples.

*

The third victim, Maria Wurlitzer (M), had been twenty at the time of the attack and a student at the university majoring in German philology and philosophy. Since her specific interests lay in the German thinkers of the eighteenth century, she soon abandoned her teenage infatuation with Hitler and developed a highly critical view of the new regime. It was, in a word, inhuman and represented a betrayal of all the Enlightenment ideals that Germany—and especially her three heroes, Johann Wolfgang von Goethe, Gotthold Ephraim Lessing, and Immanuel Kant—stood for. That little man with the little mustache would bring Europe and Germany to disaster. His militarism and war-mongering were bad enough, but his brutalization of the German soul was worse, as it portended a long period of spiritual decline that could not be overcome with a change of regimes or leaders. If centuries of cultural advancement were being destroyed, then it might take centuries for that soul to be revived, though never again in its original, glorious, humanistic form.

Hitler had to be stopped, but what could a young university student do? She had heard of something called the White Rose opposition group in Munich. Perhaps something like that would be possible in Berlin? Her best friend, Helga, an unusually busty girl who enjoyed dancing and was very popular with the boys, was outspoken in her disapproval of Hitler, especially after a glass or two of beer. She could be trusted, even if her comments occasionally skirted with outright treason. And there was the lanky brown-haired ex-Rhinelander, Robert, also a philology and philosophy major, also an admirer of Goethe, Lessing, and

Kant—and, perhaps not accidentally, of Maria as well. He, too, could be trusted.

Maria explained her views to her friends—emphasizing their moral obligation to do something to stop the madness—when they were bathing in the Wannsee one Saturday afternoon. All around them were naked young bodies, tanned and vigorous and strong. The friends had been splashing one another, but when Maria finished her well-rehearsed speech, the water turned quiet and their faces turned ashen. They knew that the conversation could mean imprisonment, but both agreed that Maria was right. Kantian morality and Lessing's and Goethe's Enlightenment humanism demanded that they do something. They finally decided that pinning anti-Nazi leaflets to lampposts, staircases, and walls was the way to proceed. The people had to know that there were critical voices, that the *Volk* was not monolithic in its love of the Führer, that moral courage had not yet perished. After they saw more and more leaflets appearing in the most unexpected corners, they would come to realize that they were not alone, that they, too, could add their voices to the rising tide of opposition, and that successful resistance was therefore possible.

The three conspirators gathered in Robert's home in Charlottenburg—his father, a high-ranking Party functionary, had acquired a spacious apartment in the aftermath of *Kristallnacht* —closed the door to his room, and set to work. Robert produced the paper, Maria composed the text, while Helga invented a handwriting that no one could mistake for hers. That evening, each of them left three copies of the leaflet on tram seats, park benches, and stairwells; the day after, Maria was arrested. Both Helga and Robert had denounced her to the Gestapo, not because they were ideological sympathizers of the regime, but because they firmly believed that only an *agent provocateur* could have dragged them into this madcap leaflet business. And they knew that the only way to defend yourself against an obvious provocation was to denounce the agent before she denounced you. Fortunately for Maria, this was her first offense. In mid-1943, she was sentenced to two years after a few beatings persuaded the police that she had acted alone. She was released several weeks before the fall of Berlin in mid-1945, tired, though not broken.

Her parents and siblings (two brothers and two sisters) were distraught by her arrest. For one thing, they had to submit to humiliating interrogations by the Gestapo. For another, they felt anger and, above all, shame that Maria should have betrayed the Führer's trust. Both brothers were in the Waffen SS (and were to die in Warsaw in late 1944, while fighting against the Polish uprising). One sister, a teenager, served actively in the *Bund Deutscher Mädel*; another, older than Maria, tended to the wounded in a hospital. "Our dead and wounded," she wrote to Maria in prison, "are on your conscience. You are their killer. You are their murderer." The words stung, both because they were so unfair and because they were not wholly inaccurate. It was true: opposition to Hitler meant opposition to the war effort and, hence, to the armed forces.

Maria's parents were both workers—and had always been workers—in nearby factories. Stefan, the father, had even been a member of the Communist Party in the late 1920s, but, for reasons he had never been able to fathom, was never identified as such when he went over to the Nazis in 1932. It wasn't opportunism that drove him to switch sides. It was the realization that the Nazi variety of socialism was likely to bring the working class more benefits, including class power, than the Soviet variety. Besides, National Socialism was German, while Soviet communism was Russian or, perhaps, even Jewish. It's not that he had anything against the Russian and Jewish comrades—he had met many at meetings, demonstrations, and parades and they were all fine fellows, though a bit too inclined to imbibe copious amounts of vodka—but it stood to reason that they were less capable of understanding the German proletariat than German National Socialists. His choice proved to be correct. Inflation fell, unemployment vanished, and a decent, normal life became possible once again—all thanks to Hitler.

Stefan worked as a lathe operator, while Leni, his wife,

supervised a team of women in a textile factory. Some of her colleagues submitted that the mother of a traitor had to have been delinquent in her parental duties and should not be supervising good German women striving to produce the best-quality clothes for the Fatherland, but Leni's membership in the Party, which she had joined before 1933, demonstrated her loyalty and silenced her critics. But her personal sense of self, like that of Stefan, had been hurt by their daughter's criminal stupidity. Father and Mother continually reminded Maria of her errant ways and of the need to reform during their visits. Her broken finger nails, parched lips, and bruised arms seemed to hint that prison conditions were less ideal than she said they were, but, although it pained them, both Stefan and Leni concurred that their daughter had no one to blame but herself for the punishment she was now justifiably receiving.

Maria, having grown wiser and more cynical in her cell, nodded in assent and, on occasion, could even manage to shed an artificial tear or two. In reality, her hatred of the regime, as well as her determination to "do something," had only intensified, all the more so as she had the opportunity to interact with equally hardened political criminals who shed light on one aspect of the regime she had not fully appreciated—that it was able to survive and thrive because it enjoyed vast popular support. When she was finally released and saw the rubble and ruins to which her city had been reduced, she wept. There was nothing left. The city was a heap of ashes. Her beloved Berlin had become a smoldering landscape of broken bricks and desperate beggars. Stunned by the destruction and rendered impotent by her weakness, she took to roaming the empty streets and trying to imagine just what had stood where before the bombs fell. It was during one such sojourn that the blond Russian had attacked her. He was ready for kicks and screams, but she was too exhausted, both spiritually and physically, and submitted without resistance and without uttering a sound. Whether her passivity excited or depressed her assailant is not clear.

*

Johanna Habermann (N) and Heidi Hardt (O), had been about forty in 1945. They were twins, born to a Bavarian couple, Franz and Elfriede Huegelmann, who worked the poor soil of Berg, a village near the northern tip of Starnberg Lake south of Munich. Ten children survived childbirth, three girls and seven boys; five did not. Maria, the eldest, and three boys emigrated to the United States in 1900, where she married a Mennonite farmer in Lancaster County, Pennsylvania, while the boys settled down in Manhattan's Yorkville neighborhood where they worked for German breweries. The other four boys all stayed on the farm and eventually, in the 1930s, volunteered for the armed forces. Three perished on various fronts, while one became a Soviet prisoner of war and was interned in a camp near Donetsk until 1953, when he returned, bedraggled, unshaven, and weighing about fifty kilograms, and found employment as a bricklayer.

The twins enjoyed the arts and the sciences, but their passion belonged to sports. They were exceptionally athletic, did well in the shorter races, and eventually joined a Bavarian team that competed in Berlin. They had hopes of taking part in the Olympics, but, being far shorter than the majestic Teutonic goddesses against whom they ran, failed their qualifying competitions and, just as Hitler came to power in early 1933, had to settle for jobs as athletic coaches in two girls' schools in the capital. They were too old to participate in the 1936 Olympic games, but both had the vicarious satisfaction of having trained several girls who did well in the qualifiers and were touted as future prospects. Unfortunately, Germany's excellent performance at the games was marred by the no less excellent performance of the American, Jesse Owens. He was exceptionally fast, they both agreed, but everyone knew that all Negroes were.

It was during the games that Johanna and Heidi had the great honor of meeting the renowned filmmaker, Leni Riefenstahl, who frequently consulted with them about matters related to performance, diet, and training. Quietly and persuasively, her film, *Olympia*, captured the essence of Germanhood—*Deutschtum*—and celebrated the emergence of the new German man and woman—healthy, vigorous, strong, and unflinching, in both body and mind. Joining the Party was the obvious next step and both did, in 1937. They remained unwavering in their commitment to National Socialist ideals throughout the war and, in fact, into the 1960s. It was only after Adolf Eichmann was tried and hanged in Israel in 1962 that both broke with an idealized past that they, as young women, had never actually known.

Their dedication to the Führer was complete. He wasn't exactly Bavarian, but his home town, Inn an der Braunau, had the good fortune of being in the south, which meant he wasn't, thank the Lord, a stiff, unsmiling, dour Prussian, didn't speak their detestable dialect, so reminiscent of canine barking, or sport an absurdly upturned mustache like the last Kaiser. Besides, his modest beginnings as leader had been in Munich and its beer halls, where the common folk congregated, and he enjoyed wearing Lederhosen. Hitler's deluded detractors couldn't understand that he was a man of the people. He spoke their language and shared their mentality. No wonder the people responded with enthusiasm to his message of reviving Germany and its honor and greatness.

The Socialists and democrats had stabbed the country in its back at the end of the last war. Were it not for them, we would have won and become a world power—a *Weltmacht*. Instead, all those poor boys died in the trenches, forests, or steppes for nothing. And who benefited? *Cui bono?* The capitalists and the Jews, who were pretty much the same. As if leading the nation to defeat weren't enough, the Reds then proceeded to guide the nation into a maelstrom of hyperinflation, unemployment, and cultural and moral collapse, while the Jews profited from the Depression and, as the common folk scrounged and starved, drank champagne and had their portraits painted! The nationalists and conservatives had no answers to Germany's ills. Only the Nazis, only Hitler, did. And, as the country's rapid revival after 1933 demonstrated, their recipes were the right ones.

The Party wasn't perfect. It went too far with its euthanasia program; its policies toward the Jews were on the whole correct, but sometimes needlessly provocative and cruel. Were the yellow stars really necessary? It was also an unquestionably good thing that the Führer had reined in the Storm Troopers in 1934 and curbed their worst excesses. As both women liked to emphasize, the essence of National Socialism was humanity and we Nazis shouldn't be afraid to show our human side. Consider the Great German Art Exhibition of 1937, which ran alongside its opposite, the Degenerate Art Exhibition. The former extravaganza showed man and woman at their best. Nazi sculpture hearkened back to ancient Greek sculpture, just as Nazi architecture was a modern German version of the genius that inspired the Parthenon. What Pericles, Solon, Philip, and Alexander began Hitler would complete. Contrast the physical and spiritual nobility conveyed by such Nazi masters as Hubert Lanzinger, Arno Breker, and Ludwig Dettmann with the crippled bodies and distorted faces of such Jews as Chagall, Picasso, Kirchner, and Kandinsky!

The war changed little in Johanna and Heidi's beliefs and attitudes toward the regime. Great Britain, France, and Russia had always been hostile to Germany and its aspirations. They surrounded us, they rattled their sabers—leaving us with no choice but to defend ourselves. The Poles were little better. Had they not attacked the Gleiwitz radio tower in the summer of 1939, the Führer would not have been impelled to resort to arms. The sly *Polaken* had lured us into war, as did, in 1941, that vile Bolshevik dictator, Stalin. What choice did we have but to defend ourselves? Could our heroic army be blamed for fighting fire with fire, for occasionally engaging in excessive use of violence? After all, the Russian hordes understood only force. Three of their brothers and both their husbands had paid the ultimate price defending the Fatherland from these savages.

As the Allied troops marched relentlessly toward Germany's heartland in 1945, both Johanna and Heidi fervently believed that, soon, very soon, a *Wunderwaffe*—a miracle weapon

—would be developed and the tide of battle would turn. When that didn't happen, despite the temporary successes achieved by the V-1 and V-2 rockets, they placed their hopes in the *Volkssturm*, the popular mobilization of young and old, men and women, in defense of the country. As Goebbels so rightly insisted, German soil is sacred and all of us must fight to the very end in defense of the Fatherland and its Führer. When Soviet tanks rumbled across the rubble of eastern Berlin and the drunken Russians descended on the defenseless people cowering in cellars and air raid shelters, the twins knew that someone, probably the Socialists who had fled to Scandinavia and betrayed their country, had once again stabbed Germany in the back.

They had been scrounging amid the bricks and glass, hunting for scraps of edible food, on the evening of the rape. Some twenty slant-eyed Russians surrounded them and ordered them to disrobe. They refused and, instead of surrendering, fought like true Aryan women. More than one Russian *Untermensch* got a black eye, broken rib, or split lip that day. In the end, the Russians overpowered them, but Johanna and Heidi had the satisfaction of demonstrating that the people, when guided by the ideas of the Führer, were invincible. One of the rapists—well, actually, several—was a blond-haired, blue-eyed boy who could have been a model member of the *Hitler Jugend*. The women remembered him because one of them had kicked him above his left eye and he had bled profusely onto their faces.

*

Bollow had no reason to doubt the women's truthfulness. They appeared not to have dwelled on exonerating details or to have concealed exceptionally heinous behaviors. That all five should have made their way to *Frauen für Frieden* made sense in light of their post-war lives. The two youngest came of age in the turbulent 1960s, when they were obviously infected by the regnant lefty dogmas of the time. Wurlitzer had always been a dissident and would have naturally gravitated toward the left. The twins both lived husbandless lives in Kreuzberg and probably joined for the company and refreshments. All in all, theirs were fairly typical German stories. These weren't self-styled heroines or self-abnegating villains. They were regular Germans who behaved in the manner of the overwhelming majority of regular Germans in the 1930s and 1940s. In a word, they collaborated.

Or did they? True, they accepted the new regime and made their peace with it. Even Maria, who tried so hard to initiate some form of organized resistance, must have known that she was engaging in a juvenile game and not the real thing. Real resistance entails violence. Distributing leaflets is just a vicarious thrill—a pretense. The two girls, Ursula and Lotte, had had girlish infatuations with a charismatic man. Who could blame them for falling under his spell? And could a ten- and thirteen-year-old be collaborators? Didn't one have to be an adult? No, only the twins came closest to collaborating, but they genuinely seemed to believe that Nazism would improve the lives of people everywhere. Theirs was an almost criminal naiveté, but could they be blamed for being overly idealistic, to the point of being sophomoric?

The case raised other disturbing questions that Bollow had earlier encountered but never fully considered. Ideally, Germans, like all people everywhere, should have fought against the Nazi dictatorship. But just how does a regular person with family and job go about resisting a dictatorship? Open protests would lead to immediate incarceration and reprisals against one's family and friends. Silent protest might enhance one's sense of moral worth, but was useless as a way of undermining the regime. Working less efficiently, deliberately making wrong decisions or mistakes was a form of semi-passive resistance, but its impact on the dictatorship would necessarily be minimal, at least in the short run. Dictators understood only force and violence, but how were ordinary Germans, who had access to neither, supposed to have acquired them? And wouldn't it have been suicidal for clerks, housewives, and librarians to have taken to arms against the Storm Troopers, SS, Gestapo, and Wehrmacht?

The selective nature of the opprobrium assigned to collaborators also troubled Bollow. Germans were roundly considered to be especially weak, especially guilty, especially responsible for the crimes of the Hitler regime. Fair enough. But the French, British, Russians, and Americans did very little to resist Hitler—and they had the military and economic wherewithal to have done so. Why didn't the French react to Hitler's seizure of the Rhineland? Why did Chamberlin give him the Sudetenland? Why did Stalin divide Poland and seize the Baltic states? Why did the Americans wait for years before invading the continent? None of them resisted in the 1930s when resistance could have nipped Hitler in the bud. Quite the contrary, they aided and abetted Hitler in his expansionist schemes. And when the Poles rose up in Warsaw in 1944, how many Europeans rushed to their assistance? And why did it occur to no one to bomb Auschwitz?

Worse, the Russians didn't even try to resist Stalin. Neither did the Czechs, Slovaks, Bulgarians, and many others. The Ukrainian, Lithuanian, Latvian, and Estonian nationalists fought Stalin—and were obliterated, their towns and villages occupied by the Soviet secret police, their populations deported to Siberia—while the freedom-loving West, which always asserted its moral superiority, did absolutely nothing. Who helped the East Germans in 1953? Or the Hungarians in 1956? Or the Czechs and Slovaks in 1968? No one, absolutely no one. Indeed, the German Socialists under Willy Brandt pursued a policy of reconciliation and détente at precisely the time that the dictatorships in the Soviet Union and Eastern Europe were cracking down on oppositionists with relentless fury.

And then, thought Bollow, there was the question of collaboration. People were collaborators only if they helped the regime pursue its ends and did so voluntarily. Although the vast majority of Germans did support Nazi attempts to make the Fatherland strong again, they decidedly did not share the Nazi regime's genocidal goals. And when Germans failed to resist with arms or confined their criticism to kitchen whispers, they did so because they had no choice but to be quiet, just as, come to think of it, the Russians had no choice but to acquiesce in Stalin's crimes. Saints resisted and, by paying for their resistance with their lives, became martyrs. The vast majority of regular folk were neither saints nor martyrs. Good or bad, that's just the way things were—in Germany and everywhere else.

Germans had become targets of universal condemnation —for good reason. At the same time, it seemed clear to Bollow that the universality of the faultfinding was also symptomatic of a deeper problem: a tacit recognition by those engaged in condemning us of their own failings, moral lapses, and criminal complicity. The world, and not just the Germans, had made Hitler possible. The world blithely committed crimes on a daily basis, be it American repression of Negroes or French reprisals in Algeria or Russian destruction of the peasantry. The Germans had become, not undeservedly, everyone's whipping boy. One could point at the bad Germans and thereby assuage one's own guilty conscience and feel morally superior.

Unfortunately, one couldn't express these reflections openly without being labeled a Nazi sympathizer and apologist. She would have to tread very, very lightly in this dangerous terrain. And the best way to do this was to elide all these questions and focus only on the facts of the story—the rapes of five women by a blond-haired, blue-eyed Russian boy who could be, and probably was, this Professor Romanoff. But was Romanoff's complicity a fact? The rapes indubitably were. The women all claimed to have been raped by a blond-haired, blue-eyed Russian who could have been an Aryan poster boy. Bollow did not doubt their having been raped, but were they all identifying the same blond-haired, blue-eyed boy?

Many Russians were, despite the Nazi caricatures depicting them as dark-haired gorillas, blond-haired and blue-eyed. And many of those Russian boys must have been part of the armed forces that liberated Berlin. Could she be sure that Romanoff was the culprit? The women's testimony was emotionally persuasive, but not conclusive, clearly not enough for a conviction in a court of law. But this wasn't a court of law; this was the press and to be convicted in the press required far less evidence. The twins maintained they had scarred their attacked above the left eye. If she could establish the existence of such a scar, no matter how tiny, the case would be stronger. But they also spoke of slant-eyed Russians, by which they no doubt meant natives of Central Asia or Siberia—and Romanoff was neither. The evidence was, as Bollow had to reluctantly admit, circumstantial and inconclusive.

Still, wasn't proving his culpability or innocence less important than arguing for their victimhood? Romanoff's sullied name would be a small price to pay for finally revealing the extent of Soviet crimes in Germany to the world. A possibly innocent American would pay the price, but, as a Harvard don well respected by his profession, he would survive and no doubt thrive, probably exploiting the incident as the centerpiece of his bestselling memoirs. Bollow didn't generally alter the facts to make for a better story, but might not a bit of truth stretching that conformed to the spirit of the story be in order?

*

As promised to Romanoff, the *Berliner Zeitung*'s Gisela Urban had begun researching the biographies of the five women accusers. Her first move was to telephone Sieglinde Bollow and ask if she would answer a few questions. Of course, Bollow replied. Did she believe the women? Yes, she did. Was she absolutely certain their stories were accurate? Bollow didn't reply directly; instead, choosing her words carefully, she said she had no reason to disbelieve them. Were their wartime biographies impeccable? Bollow said that M had actually been in the resistance. And what of K, L, N, and O? Bollow pretended not to hear and iterated her claim about M. Urban pressed the point. Did that mean the others were positively inclined to the Hitler regime? Bollow said that K and L were only children and that N and O were forgetful. Again, this evasiveness, thought Urban. That meant that four of the five almost certainly had checkered wartime pasts and that only one, M, was probably completely clean.

"Could you tell me their names?" she asked Bollow. "This anonymity is a bit ridiculous. I'll find out who they are anyway, though it'll take time." Then she added, "Next time, I'll do you a favor."

Pretending to hesitate, Sieglinde hemmed and hawed and finally agreed. Urban would be in her debt, but, more important, Gisela would be doing her a big favor by researching the women's backgrounds and corroborating their stories. Sooner or later, the world would learn of their infatuations with Hitler and Nazism and it would be better, for her and the *Berliner Zeitung*, if a future scandal concerning their pasts were to be uncovered as soon as possible. The very last thing she wanted was for this affair to capture the popular imagination and then, just as Romanoff was on the verge of being crucified, for the women's testimony to be discredited. She and her paper would be denounced, the women would be deemed gossip-mongers and liars, and her own career could be placed in jeopardy. If there were problems with their stories and their biographies, better that they should reach the public eye now, rather than later.

For her part, Urban found Bollow's all-too-ready willing-ness to help suspicious. Journalists rarely, if ever, shared their stories and their sources. True, it made sense for Bollow to aid an influential colleague who would probably uncover the same facts about the women, but Bollow's evasive answers, when combined with her excessive good will, suggested that she was not quite as certain about the women and their accusations as she let on. In all likelihood, they were hiding something. In all likelihood, they were hiding what all Germans were hiding —their relationship to the Hitler regime. Urban herself wasn't completely forthright about that aspect of her past. And she knew that Sieglinde also had something to hide. No, she in-ferred, it wasn't a question of likelihoods: although Sieglinde had depicted them as heroines in her stories, the women were definitely concealing their Nazi pasts. Only one of them, Maria Wurlitzer, was probably on the level, but her testimony would be placed in doubt by her friendship with four women who would be tarred and feathered as Nazis regardless of whether they had or had not been assaulted. Bollow's generosity now made perfect, even if predictably regrettable, sense. By drawing Ursula into the affair, by giving her unrestricted access to her sources, Sieglinde was hoping to make her guilty by association and thus equally liable to whatever possible storm might break out. How clever, how insidious—and how professional!—of her. Urban's face broke into a wide grin. This was the kind of journalism she understood.

Although Bollow's reluctant revelations probably got Romanoff off the hook, Urban decided against telling him the good news. She would say she had tried, but could unearth nothing. He would have no reason to disbelieve her. Let him squirm. The professor was an arrogant prick who regarded himself far too highly. Yes, he had accomplished much. And yes, he truly was an important historian. But three things militated against him: that he was Russian, that he was American, and that he was a Harvard professor. The Russians claimed to have liberated us, but in fact did not. The Americans did in fact liberate us, but then imposed their juvenile culture on the land of thinkers and poets. And Harvard professors were an insufferable lot who believed they had the right and obligation to teach the world.

CHAPTER THREE

Sieglinde Bollow had experienced two epiphanies in the whirlwind 1960s. Born shortly after the war, she had come of age during the years of the *Wirtschaftswunder*, the economic miracle of the 1950s that saw Germany rebound to prewar levels of prosperity. The crafty Adenauer was Chancellor and, despite his abundant jowls and wrinkled skin, seemed destined to remain in office forever, while most Germans were obsessed with satisfying their *Nachholbedarf*, or need to catch up, by aspiring to a television set, a shiny Volkswagen, and a one-week vacation in Italy. Her generation reveled in American pop culture, with the boys sporting DA haircuts modeled on Elvis or James Dean and the girls wearing bobby socks and pleated skirts. Hula hoops and transistor radios were, as she recalled, the height of fashion at one point. The war had been conveniently forgotten by most Germans, as it had by most Americans, British, and French, and most of the people who ran Germany in the 1930s and 1940s were still running it in the 1950s and 1960s. As Adenauer observed, don't pour out the brown water if you can't refill the bucket with clean water. The East Germans, Poles, Russians, and other communist nations couldn't seem to forget the war, but they didn't matter.

Sieglinde's first epiphany—it was, actually, a series of events that culminated in a change of heart and view—took place in the early to mid-1960s, when she was completing her *Abitur* degree in middle school and embarking on studies at the Free University of Berlin. The Negro civil rights movement had exposed the depth of racism in the United States. Sieglinde saw the television footage of helmeted white policemen and grinning thugs striking defenseless black demonstrators with sticks and cudgels. She watched Martin Luther King deliver his famous "I have a dream" speech at the Lincoln Memorial in Washington. In time, she would also see his death at the hands of a white racist and the explosions of black rage that shook American cities and rocked the very foundations of capitalist rule.

Meanwhile, the war in Vietnam had exposed the barbaric face of American imperialism and the exploitative economic system that sustained and promoted it. Vietnam posed no conceivable geopolitical threat to the American giant, except that its people's desire for a just society built on socialist foundations could not be tolerated by the cigar-smoking fat cats in Washington and on Wall Street who hoped to subordinate the entire world to their greed. America and its henchmen, especially such puppets as the Shah of Iran, had to be resisted. Sieglinde had taken part in the riots during the Shah's 1967 visit to Berlin, when a member of Germany's hated repressive apparatus shot and killed an innocent student, Benno Ohnesorg. Sieglinde had known Benno; the two had even had a fleeting relationship. His death was a personal affront as well as a political crime. When the charismatic student leader Rudi Dutschke proceeded to mobilize his comrades against the repressive system with his hypnotic oratory, Sieglinde joined. When he was shot and almost killed in 1968, her determination to smash the capitalist-imperialist state only increased.

It was during these turbulent years, and especially after the ex-Nazi Kiesinger became Chancellor in 1966, that Sieglinde, like so many others of her generation, asked her parents a simple question: "What did you do during the war?" The question was obvious, but it had never occurred to her to ask it before. Now it seemed like the only question worth asking. After all, the German system was full of former Nazis. Nothing had changed since Hitler's death and the country's defeat in the war. If the people who ran fascist Germany in the 1930s and 1940s were still in power, then it followed that the country, even today, was still fascist and had to be transformed immediately.

Her parents, when confronted with that question,

equivocated and Sieglinde knew they had something to hide. Her nagging finally bore fruit. Her father, a lawyer, had served in the Ministry of Justice. Her mother, a writer of children's books, had published a series illustrating the poisonous influence of Jews and other *Untermenschen* on German children. He insisted he had nothing to do with the arrests and deportations of Jews, political prisoners, and other undesirables. "I was a paper pusher," he pleaded. "They gave me documents and I filled them out and passed them along." When pressed to describe the documents in greater detail, he would invoke memory lapses and reassuringly say that they were "just regular documents, nothing special, absolutely nothing incriminating." His protestations struck her as being excessive, so, after some digging in the archives, she discovered that her father had investigated "economic crimes" committed by wealthy Jews about to leave the country. Expropriations followed and Sieglinde wondered whether the small Picasso print that hung on the living room wall was not perhaps the illicit product of one of these expropriations. Her father claimed to have bought it at a flea market.

Her mother had no excuses, which was a relief. They paid her well and she had to admit that some of the anti-Semitic propaganda had rubbed off on her: "I am not excusing myself, dear Sieglinde, but you must understand that the economy, the culture, the arts—they were all in the hands of the Jews. It was easy to believe they were responsible for all our ills." When Sieglinde asked her how she felt drawing caricatures of Jewish children with long hooked noses and side locks, her mother just shook her head slowly and whispered, "Badly, though you must understand that they really did look that way." It slowly dawned on Sieglinde that her mother's lack of excuses was her excuse.

The realization that both her parents had contributed to National Socialism had been a shock. True, they hadn't pulled any triggers and they hadn't consigned any people to concentration camps, but they had actively supported the regime and directly participated in and sustained its system of rule. Things were even worse with her relatives. Two uncles had served in the

SS and been de-Nazified in the immediate aftermath of the war. One aunt had worked in the German film industry and collaborated with Ernst von Salomon on screenplays. They were Hollywood-type kitsch stories, but, even so, her complicity in the regime's propaganda apparatus was damnable. A few aunts and uncles appear to have done nothing but keep their heads low, but none had resisted in any sense of the word. Sieglinde Bollow would, however, even if it meant breaking all ties to her family.

*

Sieglinde's second epiphany came after Andreas Baader took to fire-bombing department stores in Frankfurt and was arrested in 1970. He said he had been protesting "the public's indifference to the genocide in Vietnam" and, while sympathetic to his cause, Sieglinde realized with the clarity of a convert that she rejected the means. If there were to be change, even radical change, it would have to come about through non-violent or minimally violent means. Her relatives and parents had contributed enough to the brutalization of German society; they had normalized violence by making it appear to be a legitimate way of conducting politics. There might be times that made violence necessary—Sieglinde was no pacifist—but it was to be eschewed for as long as possible until it became, literally, the very last resort. Baader, like Meinhof and Ensslin, had made the mistake of thinking that capitalist violence justified anti-capitalist violence. It did not. King was right, as was Gandhi.

Once she rejected Germany's violent left, it was probably only a matter of time before Sieglinde would come to realize that working through the system, no matter how unjust it was or seemed to be, was the only way to bring about ethically justified radical change. It would be a "long march through the institutions," as other radicals-turned-moderates described the journey before them, but it was the only kind of march that post-war Germans who acknowledged their responsibility for Hitler's crimes could pursue. She began writing investigative articles and opinion pieces for a variety of local outlets. Eventually, she received a call from the Springer paper. They had seen her work and liked it. She had an independent mind and a good pen and they were hoping to have her join their staff of full-time reporters with excellent health benefits and no strings attached. Sieglinde wasn't certain about the absence of strings, but figured this was a good way to put her ideas and ideals to practice and try to make the difference so critical to her generation's sense of self.

Her perceptions of Berlin changed as well. The outpost of socialism now became an outpost of the West. The Wall, which she had regarded as a protective measure adopted by an East German regime under pressure from imperialism, now struck her as a violation of the city's integrity and spirit. The Socialists had degenerated into naïve fellow travelers of the Soviet regime and were unacceptable. The Christian Democrats, though still unappealing in so many ways, had thereby become palatable as a political alternative, especially after Günter Guillaume, Chancellor Willy Brandt's personal assistant, had been exposed as a long-time Communist spy and Brandt was forced to resign in May 1974. Was it possible that Ostpolitik was developed and promoted by the Soviet secret police?

The two Germanys sat on the front line of the Cold War and, as much as she hated to admit it, Germans had to choose sides. You were either with the East Germans and the Soviet Union or you were with the West Germans and the United States. There were times when Sieglinde longed for a third way, but she knew that, in given circumstances, it was an illusion. Even Tito's Yugoslavia, which claimed to have invented non-alignment and a third way, was far more entangled with the West than with the East. The wily Yugoslav leader knew where he'd be more likely to remain independent enough to pursue his national road to socialism. The Hungarians and Czechoslovaks had known that as well and paid the price of having to endure Soviet invasions in 1956 and 1968. And, naturally, the Soviets knew full well that there was no third way as long as they had anything to say about it.

Sieglinde had little love for the United States, its preposterous people, and their vulgar culture, but she felt only repulsion when it came to the socialist states in the East—and above all the USSR. Their goose-stepping soldiers on Red Square, their aged and dull leadership, their brutal interventions throughout the world, and their inability to create minimally decent societies in the lands they occupied were damning evidence of the Soviets' illfittedness for rule. The capitalists had their many faults, but at least the countries they ran worked—sometimes quite well—and life was, on the whole, tolerable for most people. How many Americans sought political asylum in Russia? And how many Soviets would gladly jump ship if they suspected they wouldn't get shot crossing No Man's Land and breaching the Wall? Only the West Germans were, still, stupid and naïve enough to believe that they didn't have to take sides in the Cold War. That was just a preposterous affectation, a way of asserting their cultural superiority and, hence, symptomatic of the mindset that made Hitler possible. As distasteful as the Americans were, they were the only choice.

*

According to Gisela Urban's conversations with the twins, they had contacted Sieglinde Bollow on the same day that Romanoff's interview had appeared in the *Berliner Zeitung*. Despite their advanced age, Johanna and Heidi went straight to the editorial offices, planted themselves in easy chairs, demanded coffee, and waited for her. They trusted her, they said. Her articles were balanced and measured and she seemed to be committed to the truth. They had, they said, a terrible confidence to impart to her, something that neither of them had revealed to the world—or even to their husbands, God bless them. It was during the Soviet occupation of Berlin, in May 1945, to be exact, that both of them were victims of gang rapes by slant-eyed Russians. Sieglinde had raised her eyebrows upon hearing their statement, but more out of politeness than surprise. All Berliners, even those on the far left, knew about the mass rapes, so this was nothing new and most definitely not news.

The next sentence uttered by one of the twins came as a shock. They claimed to know who the perpetrator was. "How could you know that?" Sieglinde demanded. "Did you see his papers or learn his name?" No, they replied, he was here in Berlin —*now, right now*—and his interview had just appeared in the *Berliner Zeitung*, at which point both proceeded to withdraw crumpled copies of the newspaper from their handbags and hand them to Sieglinde. Bollow had read the interview over breakfast and been unimpressed by the American scholar of Russian descent. She had no use for his arcane theories or for his archival work and she certainly had no intention of ever reading any of his famous books, whether in the original or in translation. But the accusations shed a different light on this unprepossessing professor of history.

"Are you sure he was the one?" she asked. "Are you absolutely sure?"

"Of course, we are," they replied in a huff. "Why else would we be here?"

"But how can you be absolutely sure about something that took place thirty years ago under conditions of chaos?" she persisted.

"Have you ever been raped?" one of them enquired. "If you had, you'd know that one cannot ever forget."

Maybe yes, maybe no, reckoned Sieglinde, *vielleicht ja, vielleicht nein*, but there was nothing she could say in response without appearing to be insensitive to the women's very real suffering. Both had tears in their eyes and both spoke amid sniffling and delicate handkerchief dabs to their cheeks. Could this be a set up? But why would two pensioners decide to exact revenge on some Harvard professor? Whatever the case, she would have to look into it, if only because of the political implications if the charges were true.

One of the twins then dropped another bombshell. They weren't alone in their accusations. There were three other women who would testify that this Professor Romanoff had in fact been the blond-haired, blue-eyed Russian boy who had raped them all in 1945. Either Johanna or Heidi proceeded to name them and briefly describe their backgrounds. "How did you find out about them?" Sieglinde asked. "By accident," one twin replied. They were all members of the *Frauen für Frieden* and had, in the course of the last few years, shared some personal stories. As it turned out, all had been raped by the Russians. It was only after the interview and photographs appeared that morning that they all recognized their rapist. They called one another—and, "well, here we are."

"And you're sure, you're absolutely—" Sieglinde interrupted herself in mid-sentence. "Of course, you are." She paused to consider what her next step should be. "I need to speak to my editor. Please wait here." They could see that she was struggling to hide a hint of a smile. "This is sensational. *Vielen Dank*—many thanks."

The editor agreed that the story was sensational and promised to give it page-one coverage. Unfortunately, he also copyedited her draft, chose the headlines, and included much of the lurid language that so disturbed Romanoff. Bollow had some qualms, but she had been in the business long enough to know that screaming headlines sold newspapers. There was no point to writing tempered articles if no one read them.

As she reviewed her notes, Urban easily identified the weak link in these accounts. Did the women simultaneously recognize the photograph of Romanoff, in which case they could claim to be five independent witnesses? Or did one of them convince the others, either after the interview appeared or well before it, to point their fingers at some blond-haired, blue-eyed Russian who could have been Romanoff or someone with slanted eyes? That four of the five also had checkered pasts didn't help, as it pointed to the not unreasonable deduction that they were hoping to minimize their guilt by claiming victimhood. Small wonder, Urban wryly concluded, that Sieglinde was hoping to drag me into this swamp.

*

Bollow was surprised that she was the only journalist to attend Romanoff's unsuccessful press conference. They had assembled some thirty uncomfortable chairs and, even fifteen minutes after the announced start of the event, only one, hers, was occupied. Romanoff stood awkwardly on the sidelines, smoking and casting nervous glances at his watch and the unresponsive door every few seconds. But, despite his agitation, no one came and, thirty minutes later, one of his colleagues came to the microphone, mumbled, "Today's press conference has been cancelled for, er, obvious reasons," and slunk off.

It was unfortunate that Romanoff probably came away with the impression that she was a witch—what with the banner headlines and excessive use of question marks and exclamation points in her articles. It was true that she said, "What do you have to hide, *Herr Doktor*?" after the event was cancelled. But the tone wasn't snide or, in any case, the snideness was not directed against the professor, as he no doubt believed. Rather, it was directed against herself. The press conference was a waste of time and, instead of sitting there waiting for someone else to show up, Sieglinde knew she should have politely excused herself and gone home immediately. But this one-on-one confrontation that was no real confrontation grated on her nerves, reminding her that she had suddenly found herself in an awkward controversy that risked ruining her reputation as well as his. Staring at Romanoff from beneath her brow and seeing that he was returning the stare, Sieglinde realized that this was no mere story about an important, if forgotten, series of events thirty years ago. No, this was a scandal, a controversy, a case, or, as the Germans said, a *Fall*, and such things never ended well for any of their participants.

Romanoff had looked mousy in the photographs printed by the *Berliner Zeitung*. But, seeing him in the flesh, wearing a navy-blue three-piece suit, crisply ironed white shirt, a striped silk tie, and gleaming black Oxfords suggested that she was dealing with a very different kind of professor. Above all, he was young and radiated vigor. His hair was blond (was that proof of his complicity?), his eyes were blue—a sparkling blue that Sieglinde found mesmerizing (more proof?)—his nose was sleek and straight, his chin was strong, and his lips were thin, though that could have been the result of his annoyance. The man, at forty-five or so, was attractive, in his masculine prime. Harvard's female professors and graduate students must have found him irresistible. For a moment Bollow closed her eyes and imagined him drinking wine with some leggy history major in an inn on Cape Cod. No, that would be too easy and too gauche. The woman would be a recently tenured professor of Russian literature determined to enjoy the good life now that she had become a permanent fixture in Cambridge. She opened her eyes. This had to stop. The professor was possibly a monster, even if a debonair one. Before she left, she asked Romanoff for an interview. He stared at her eyes and then flinched slightly before giving her his hotel number.

Whether he actually meant to give her the interview Bollow did not know, but she was determined to try. She had to give his side of the story, even if suitably redacted and peppered with appropriate commentary. There were, she had been taught by those of her colleagues influenced by American practices, always two sides to every controversy and journalists were supposed to swallow their political and ideological preferences and attempt to strike something resembling a balance. Most German, indeed, most European, journalists were rather less committed to this ideal of supposed objectivity, believing that one had to take sides for the good of the cause. Which cause? Well, that depended. That varied with the newspaper and the journalist. Everyone had his point of view and there was no reason to conceal it. Quite the opposite, state it up front and splice it into the entire fabric of your account, though preferably in a manner that doesn't come across as crude propaganda.

Was Romanoff's side of the story worth printing? He would think so, but would it be fair to the five women for their accounts to be denied in the very same newspaper that first published them? Would justice be more or less likely? There was no telling in advance. She would do the interview—or, more accurately, offer the prospect of an interview to Romanoff and let him decide whether he wanted to do it or not. Then, assuming she had it, she would let her editor decide whether to run it or not. Distancing herself from the ultimate decision to run it was somewhat cowardly, but being relieved of the moral burden of resisting or collaborating with this particular enemy was worth a hint of shame.

Naturally, her editor found the interview to be a *wunderbare Idee*. She then dialed Romanoff, gingerly and with a trembling hand, and, to her grief and relief—she wasn't sure which emotion was stronger—he promptly said yes. They agreed to meet for dinner in an out-of-the-way Turkish restaurant in Kreuzberg. Berlin's affluent or powerful elites rarely set foot in that neighborhood, an enclave tucked up against the Wall with dilapidated housing stock inhabited by poor immigrants and long-haired *Alternativler* searching for an alternative to bourgeois life amid people with no comprehension of or sympathy for their aspirations.

*

The picketers were out in full force as Bollow exited the glass and steel building that housed her newspaper. There were usually no fewer than ten; sometimes, as today, the number could reach as many as thirty, half of whom were young women, recognizable primarily by their beardless faces. They carried signs and chanted, protesting, among other things, against Springer's alleged war-mongering, U.S. imperialism, the nuclear arms race, and world hunger, though never against Soviet transgressions. Sieglinde always took their leaflets, perhaps because of some misplaced sense of politeness or because they reminded her of her own naïve activism a decade ago. She and the demonstrators even had their preassigned roles.

"*Wie geht's?*" she would ask them. "What's up?"

"All's well," they'd beam back. "The struggle against your boss continues."

"Good luck!" she'd respond and wave good-bye with a leaflet.

This time, however, Sieglinde couldn't resist ad-libbing a question: "And what does the revolution think about the five rape victims?"

No immediate response was forthcoming, until a Rudi Dutschke look-alike gruffly shouted, *"Faschistische Propaganda!"* The others joined in a chorus of denunciations: *"Schande! Schande! Schande!"*

Surprised that her wisecrack about the revolution had sparked such venomous accusations—and of just what have I to be ashamed?—Bollow let an evanescent half-smile glide across her lips, nodded for reasons she couldn't comprehend, mumbled an inaudible *Auf Wiedersehen,* and flew across the square to the taxi stand. Seeing the professor would almost come as a relief, she decided, as she gave the cab driver the directions.

Sieglinde arrived early, some fifteen minutes before the arranged time of her meeting with Romanoff. They had purposely chosen six o'clock, thereby giving themselves a good two hours before the place began to fill up. She ordered a drink and headed for a corner table in the back, shielded on two sides by walls and by an unnecessary plant on the third. They'd be almost invisible and no casual diner would likely adduce that the two main players in an unfolding scandal were dining together. The waiter, a fawning smile pasted below his disheveled mustache, bowed as he approached the table with a raki; as she poured it into the water and watched it turn a chalky white, she almost laughed out loud. Here was a precise image of her current circumstances. Everything had been clear and easy; it was now about to become murky and complex. I have a bad feeling about this, she thought. I have probably set a trap for myself. This Romanoff is no idiot. He will twist and turn like an eel and pervert the meaning of words to the point that they lose all meaning and nothing will appear to be what it is—or was. Was he a postmodernist? she wondered. If so, she was in for quite a ride. It occurred to her that she should leave. Who needed the stupid interview anyway? She placed the raki on the table, pushed back her chair, and grabbed her bag. And then she heard Romanoff's smooth voice say, "Hello, *Fräulein* Bollow? May I join you?" He was smiling graciously and handing her a rose.

"*Frieden?*" he asked. "Peace?"

A smooth operator: was that a proposal or a question? She smiled back and said, "Yes, please sit down." His sincerity struck her as being too sincere, but his charm was undeniable. And the man *was* attractive.

Romanoff was impeccably polite in the old-school European way that was going rapidly out of fashion. His mouth was large, some might even say luscious, revealing a gleaming set of teeth. His fingers—she noticed the fingers immediately—were long and thin: they were a pianist's fingers. He spoke softly, occasionally cocking his head to the left, as if in some confusion. He barraged her with questions about herself, her life, her education, her profession, never interrupting, never disputing the veracity of something she related, at most tilting his head quizzically. As she rattled on and on about something she no longer remembered and, as he listened or pretended to listen—a rare male character trait that she found irresistible from her commune days, when the men would preen by talking endlessly of contradictions and class struggle—Sieglinde had an epiphany: she knew she would sleep with him tonight. That would be completely irresponsible of her, indeed, it was completely crazy —*ganz verrückt*—but everything about this assignment was *ganz verrückt.* So, why not tempt fate? Why not push things past the limits of rationality and see what happened? Besides, if he was a rapist, she just might find some conclusive evidence of that in his love-making technique. Wouldn't she be courting disaster, a possible rape? No, she decided, that would be the very last thing he could afford to do in these precarious circumstances. He would have to be as polite in his love-making as he was in his dinner conversation.

After some thirty or forty minutes, she abruptly stopped and produced an embarrassed grin. "I've been talking too long," she murmured apologetically, *"Entschuldigung."* No need for apologies, he said, his contorted lips struggling to cross the silent void that had emerged between them. She coughed, drank some water, and coughed again, whereupon he cleared his throat and, leaning toward her, produced what sounded like an official denial: "No, I did not." Confused by this unexpected turn in their conversation, Sieglinde glanced up from her plate and studied his face. Nothing twitched. His eyes were focused on hers. He looked and sounded sincere. Too sincere?

"I was here," he continued. "As a boy, as a blond-haired, blue-eyed boy. And yes," his eyes focused on hers, "I knew of the rapes. I saw them with my own eyes. And perhaps, if I had been older and more experienced, if I had been less terrified of being killed by a sniper or blown to pieces by a booby trap, if I had been less of a boy, who knows? Perhaps I, too, would have participated." A long pause followed and Sieglinde couldn't decide whether it was intentional or not. "But I did not." He spoke sadly, slowly, as if in a confessional. "We hated you Germans. No, hate isn't the right word. It was more than hate. It was some kind of visceral feeling in the gut and heart and soul."

"We deserved it," she said softly.

"Perhaps, but that's not my point. That hatred was everywhere—in us, outside of us, all around us. We were its servants—no, we were its slaves. It possessed us completely." He hesitated as if unable to recall some distant event. "Did you ever read that poem—'Kill Him'—by one of our major hack poets, Konstantin Simonov?" She shook her head. "It's dreadful, the worst possible propaganda. But the sentiment was genuine. One of the stanzas describes a rape by three Germans of one's sweetheart. We experienced that. We witnessed it. And we could do nothing about until Stalingrad. Then the tables turned and it was our turn to kill."

"And to rape?"

"And to rape. But most of all to kill. Do you know how the

poem ends? 'Kill him! Kill him! Kill!' How's that for genteel verse? Can you believe it? I still know it by heart."

"But the women were innocent."

"Quite," he replied, "except that they, too, were Germans and no Germans were completely—"

She finished his sentence: "innocent."

"Exactly."

"But neither were the women completely guilty, surely not as guilty as the SS, the Gestapo…"

"Which is why the rapes were war crimes." He looked her directly in the eyes again. "They weren't spontaneous, you know. The officers gave us the wink and the nod. It was policy. The point was to rape Germany in the same way that the Germans had raped Russia. Most of the soldiers were more than happy to comply."

"But there were children and grandmothers among the victims!"

"As there were in Russia." He withdrew a sleek silver case from his pocket, removed a cigarette, tapped it against the table, placed it above the flame of the candle until it caught fire, and took a long drag. "Look, Sieglinde—excuse me, may I call you Sieglinde?" She nodded. "I am not trying to excuse this behavior, only to explain it. Remember: I am a historian. I am in the business of dealing with wars, massacres, and genocides, of trying to place them within some kind of comprehensible historical narrative, of making sense of man's universal proclivity to act toward his fellow human beings as a vicious beast. *Homo homini lupus*, right? The Germans were swine, but so, too, were the Russians. As well as the Americans and the French and the British and everybody else. It wasn't you who obliterated Hiroshima and Nagasaki. It wasn't you who captured Moscow in 1812. It wasn't you who destroyed millions of Africans and Asians in colonial adventures."

"Our colonies were short-lived, but our brutality was no less than theirs," she explained, both apologizing and meekly protesting against her need to apologize.

"Please don't misunderstand me," he continued, ignoring her intervention. "I am not trying to apologize for Hitler or Stalin or their soldiers and policemen. It's just that it's impossible for students of history not to reach the conclusion that all of mankind is capable of the worst kinds of crimes—always and everywhere." This time, Romanoff opted for a brief pause and then resumed his monologue. "Did you ever read the Old Testament?" She shook her head. "You should. It's a story of unrelieved killing. The Jews kill their enemies, slaughter their animals, and raze their buildings. Their enemies respond in kind —or try to. And God—yes, God—is the greatest killer of them all." Now Romanoff shook his head. "What chance, then, for humanity to be any different from their Maker?"

He rubbed out his cigarette in the ashtray and scrutinized her plaintively, with an expression of despair and hopelessness commingled with a touch of defiance. "I killed Germans, you know," he said. "I don't even know how many, but I know there were many—very many, possibly hundreds. We shot them even as they raised their hands in surrender and waved white rags...." His voice trailed off momentarily. "I have blood on my hands. See?" He raised and turned them slowly. "But I am no rapist."

He lit another cigarette and turned to Sieglinde. "Let me ask you a question. And no evasions, please. You are not a journalist and I am not a professor now. We are just two human beings—two confused human beings."

"Well?" she demanded impatiently.

"Is violence ever justified?"

"Of course—in self-defense."

"Exactly!" he cried. "Though how German of you to be so —do you know the American word, wishy-washy?"

"Perhaps," she replied, ignoring his jibe, "but that doesn't make me wrong."

"I assume you'll agree that we Russians were defending ourselves and had every right to resist with violence." She nodded. "And that we had a right to be as brutal as we needed to be in order to defend the Motherland." He resumed his explanation after her nodding stopped and a second or two had passed. "So, did I have a right to fire bullets into the heads of defenseless Germans? I was defending my country, wasn't I?"

She sensed a trap and, evasively, said, "It depends."

"On what?"

"On your state of mind. Were you doing it out of pleasure or were you doing it because you felt there was no other choice?"

"The latter, naturally."

"Naturally."

"Now, here's the problem. Sustained killing affects one's soul. Women, fortunately, don't understand that because no society forces them to pick up arms and kill in its defense. Men, on the other hand, are all too familiar with the problem of killing. I kill once and my conscience hurts and gives me no respite. I kill twice and that conscience appears slightly dulled. By the time I've killed my hundredth German, my conscience is dormant and killing has become transformed—from something exceptional and horrible to something commonplace and natural. By the time I've killed my five-hundredth German, shooting them in the back of their heads, especially when their hands are raised high, begins to look like an act of mercy. And by the time I'm done killing my thousandth German, raping his wife or mother or daughter or child looks like nothing more than an unwilling act of self-defense."

"Your logic is twisted," Bollow countered, fearing that she had stepped onto a slippery slope. "You are being Jesuitical."

"Now, now," he smiled graciously, "let us leave the good Jesuits out of this." His demeanor turned serious again and he hesitated briefly, in order to create the impression of uncertainty before going for the kill. "The logic is the product of war and the killing it forces us to engage in," he stated peremptorily. "What we call war crimes and atrocities are nothing more than the logical consequences of war. There will always be the former as long as there is the latter." He leaned back and exhaled a perfectly formed ring of smoke. "Remember what the infamous Simonov wrote about saving our wives and mothers from the

Germans:

> *Know that no one will save her*
> *If you don't save her.*
> *Know that no one will kill him*
> *If you don't kill him."*

"Then humanity will never be able to escape this spiral of destruction and self-destruction…" Was she protesting or apologizing?

"There may be a solution"—his eyes were twinkling —"and it may lie in your hands." Puzzled by his cryptic remark, she raised her hand defensively to her lips. "Women should serve on the front lines together with men. They should kill and they should be killed just as we kill and are killed." The twinkle had vanished. Was he being serious or merely provocative, hoping to throw her off balance?

"But that would spell the end of civilization!" she protested, sensing she had no choice but to be genuinely outraged by his proposition. "We would all become brutes."

"Or it would force us all to realize that the only way to end the brutality engendered by war is to end war. Who knows? Perhaps you women would discover ways of ending the slaughter if it affected you as much as it affects men. We haven't done a very good job. Maybe you'd do better."

"Or worse," she said gloomily, her thoughts momentarily focused on Meinhof and Ensslin, "or much, much worse."

"In which case we will all die making love in the trenches. See? Ultimately, like you, I am an optimist and an idealist!"

How did one respond to that? For want of anything better, Sieglinde said, "Let's go. It's getting crowded."

"To the trenches?" he asked, his eyebrows raised quizzically. Was he propositioning her? Or was he just being coy? There was only one way to find out.

*

A milky light seeped into the room through the jagged cracks between the shades and the window frame. The alarm clock ticked loudly. Her cat, which always shared her bed, was probably hiding in some closet. Sieglinde watched Romanoff's face as he slept. He seemed barely to breathe and, were it not for the occasional twitching of his eyelashes, he could have been a corpse. She had been struck before by the coldness of his skin. Was it reflective of his emotional condition? That would explain a lot.

His peroration on violence and war had terrified her with its cold-blooded, though not unpersuasive, logic. He appeared to be a man who had done genuine evil in war. And he had effectively argued that the evil he had done was not his fault, but war's. Fair enough, but where, then, was there room in this argument for human will, for choice? If killing inured us to killing, if violence inured us to violence, then men and women were mere pawns of history. He'd say that that's precisely what soldiers were, through no fault of their own. They were robbed of their individuality and capacity to choose freely, on the legitimate grounds that war required absolute obedience, and then compelled to collect scalps. How could such brutalization not produce brutality? Perhaps forcing women to be soldiers would enhance humanity's reluctance to resort to war. We would probably suffer intolerably high casualties and insist on suing for peace. Our children would go unattended and grow up as savages. Societies would fray and both men and women might realize they needed to dispense with violence completely. Or, more likely than not, Armageddon would ensue.

Her musings returned to the sleeping professor. The seduction hadn't quite gone according to plan. Romanoff had insisted on accompanying her to her home, a spacious apartment in Charlottenburg located on the fourth floor of a late nineteenth-century building outfitted with high ceilings and marble balconies and overlooking Lietzen Lake. They had taken a taxi along the dismal streets, with him sitting in the front and her in the back. He then paid the driver, gave him a far-too-generous tip, accompanied her to her door, and was ready to say his good-byes, when she suggested a nightcap, a spot of cognac perhaps, and, after a second's hesitation, he had agreed. She drank hers in a few minutes, while he coddled his glass, looked about uncertainly, and took occasional sips. She joined him on the couch and placed her hand on his, drawing it to her thigh, and felt a momentary reluctance, followed by the expected acquiescence. That was the signal, obviously, but he failed to respond, so, after a few moments of awkwardness, she pushed him back and pressed her body against his. He lay back stiffly, watching with what appeared to be bemusement as she removed her blouse and bra and began undoing his trousers. The expected tumescence wasn't there. Romanoff seemed manifestly embarrassed by the whole proceeding, mumbled some barely audible apology about not being in the mood, and rolled out from under her, leaving her lying, absurdly, half-naked on her own sofa. Yes, the seduction had done everything but go according to plan. She couldn't resist giggling, which only enhanced his embarrassment; the awkwardness was finally dispelled somewhat when he poured two cognacs, handed her a sniffer, and they drank the contents in one swift gulp.

"We could," he tendered, "just lie in an embrace—and whisper sweet nothings."

"Or *not*," she countered, irritated by his smooth transition from seeming sincerity to insufferable irony and deciding that she preferred to conduct a silent conversation with herself for the rest of the night.

They soon fell asleep, in their clothes and in the absence of any conversation, whether silent or not. And now here she was, studying this strange man and wondering whether he was *schwul*. Having actively partaken in the free-love practices of the communes she had inhabited in the 1960s, Sieglinde had come to view the giving and taking of sex as a commonplace activity, a perfectly natural, even mundane exchange of services, emotions, bodily fluids, and body parts. She had yet to meet a man who could resist her charms, especially when freely offered. As a matter of fact, hers hadn't been just freely offered. They had been imposed on Romanoff. She had pushed him back and thrown herself on him. What man could not be excited by such sublime lack of subtlety? A *Schwuler* could—possibly. She observed Romanoff's placid face. Was this beautiful man really gay? He didn't exude the brash masculinity of a Baader, but there was nothing about him to typecast him as anything but a heterosexual. Except, perhaps, the willowy pianist's fingers and ivory teeth.

There was another, more flattering, possibility. Romanoff could be impotent. Some men were, as she well knew from the communes, where male bravado frequently concealed an inability to perform—not well, but at all. A war wound, a psychological scar, some brutalizing experience might have done it for Romanoff. Or it could have been a series of rapes that he witnessed or committed. Wasn't it possible that they had the long-term effect of distorting his psyche and sense of self and producing an inability to engage in the act that caused the trauma in the first place? Possibly—or just as possibly she was engaging in amateurish psychologizing without any basis in reality or theory.

His jacket hung on the back of a chair near the bed. She lowered her legs slowly and shuffled noiselessly toward it. His wallet was in the breast pocket. Feeling like a thief, she removed it and made for the bathroom, where she switched on the light and examined its contents. Some German marks, a few credit cards, a Harvard ID card—and a torn black-and-white photograph of a strikingly handsome young man with wavy blond hair, penetratingly coal-like eyes, curved lashes, and a firm mouth. A lover? A brother? A friend? Perhaps Romanoff's father? She replaced the wallet in the pocket and returned to bed. Romanoff hadn't moved, lying still as a corpse.

Again, that dreadful image! She never compared people to corpses and here, for reasons she couldn't fathom, she had made that terrible comparison twice. Romanoff slept peacefully, so he couldn't be the source of the image. It had to come from within her soul. There was a nervousness within her, a bad feeling, a premonition of something. Women's intuition? Perhaps. She had felt the same way before her meeting with Romanoff. The planned seduction was supposed to assuage that feeling of dread, but, instead, its catastrophic and deeply embarrassing denouement only deepened the angst. How could he sleep so peacefully? How could he be oblivious of the impending disaster she sensed with all her being?

She brought her face as closely as possible to his and listened. Yes, he was breathing, though so soundlessly as to suggest he had ceased to live. His eyelashes twitched like tiny butterflies. His beautiful unkissable mouth remained closed to her interventions. His forehead, as broad as a gravestone—oh, again that terrible image!—shone in the half-light seeping through the curtains.

And then she froze. There, above his eyebrow, was a tiny scar. Yes, it was definitely a scar, just the kind one could get from a swift kick to the forehead. Her heart pounding rapidly, her breath frozen, her fingers trembling, she placed her hands to her mouth and emitted a silent shriek of triumph. The scar was above the right eye! It was above the right eye and not, as the twins had insisted, above the left eye! *Schwul* or not, her beautiful Serge was vindicated!

She closed her eyes and immediately fell asleep. When she awoke, Romanoff was gone, but he had left a note: "*Liebe Sieglinde! Entschuldigung und vielen, vielen Dank für Deinen Verständnis. Auf ein baldiges Wiedersehen—Dein Serge.*" She caught the incorrectly declined adjective preceding *Verständnis*. The professor's German was excellent, but not without mistakes—unless he purposely made them in order to create an impression of vulnerability. Was his Russian, which he had stopped speaking with natives thirty years ago, equally flawed? Had it acquired the peculiarities of émigré speak, a language that consisted of anachronistic expressions and an admixture of foreign words that she encountered whenever conversing with Americans of German descent? He had called her "dear" and signed off as "your

Serge". He had apologized and thanked her very, very much for "her understanding." (Her understanding of what? she thought. Of his not being able to get it up?) And he had ended with a wish that they see each other again soon. Was this a promise of another meeting or a polite way of saying good-bye? She had no idea. The Russians were inscrutable and the Americans were incomprehensible. And *Schwule*—gays—were worst of all.

Meanwhile, there was the story to pursue. Whatever the circumstances, another meeting with Romanoff was unavoidable. Yesterday, she realized, she had done all the talking—and if his plan had been to learn about her, he had succeeded fabulously. Next time, he would have to do the talking, not just about his wartime experiences, but about his life in Russia, his escape to the West, and his career at Harvard. She needed a Plan B. If the weight of the evidence condemned Romanoff, then she had a story. If it proved equivocal, as the scar suggested it might, she needed to be able to salvage her mission by writing a series of articles about the vile calumnies directed against a respectable Harvard professor by vengeful Nazi harpies. Her editor would be assuaged and the damned Americans would be delighted.

CHAPTER FOUR

omanoff had sensed that something wasn't quite right when, after leaving Sieglinde's apartment at daybreak and ordering a muddy espresso at a nearby café that catered to guest workers and drunks, he had instinctively grabbed for his wallet in his left breast pocket and found that it was in the right one. That was odd. His suspicions were confirmed when he opened the wallet and discovered that the photograph of his brother was in the wrong compartment. Evidently, she had rummaged among his things while he had slept. Which, come to think of it, made perfect sense.

The whole evening had obviously been a set-up, everything from the out-of-the-way restaurant, the corner table sheltered from the curious views of other customers, her proposal that he accompany her upstairs, and, above all, her surprisingly crude attempt at seducing him. A Russian woman, or even an American one, would have known that assault was no way to win favor with a gentleman. To the contrary, it was what the Americans so colorfully called a turn-off. Exactly. His desires, however incipient they may have been, had been wholly turned off by her awkward push and lunge. It occurred to him that she had effectively engaged in what some courts of law might consider attempted rape. The tables had turned with a vengeance! He laughed at the irony, one worthy of a contrived plot line. Indeed, this whole misadventure with the women and the journalist had come to resemble an airport paperback. Would it turn out happily for the protagonist or not? He laughed again as he realized he wasn't even sure who the protagonist and who the antagonist was.

He turned down Kantstrasse and headed for his hotel. A

brisk walk would do him good and clear his muddled head. Berlin was just awakening from its gray slumber. The neat storefronts were still shuttered and the cars and buses and trams were only beginning to clatter down otherwise empty, and immaculately asphalted, streets. Most visible at this time of day were the *Ausländer*—the diminutive foreign workers who distributed glossy advertisements and newspapers or scurried to the affluent neighborhoods where they tended to the gardens, cleaned the villas, and changed the diapers of the future German elite. The Turkish and Yugoslav men viewed him with unconcealed curiosity, probably suspecting that he was returning home from an all-night party or drinking bout. The women avoided his eyes and kept theirs focused on the no less immaculately asphalted sidewalks, almost as if they were determined to hunt down every errant cigarette butt.

Bollow's strategy was transparently obvious. She had hoped to elicit some indiscreet details in the course of her attempt to charm him in the restaurant—why else would she have prattled on incessantly about herself?—and, after he refused to consume too much alcohol, to use the oldest trick in the book, sex, to open him up. Her plan failed, but only because his awareness of the real motive behind her every move had amused him, rendering him immune to her blandishments. Which were ample and, in other circumstances, would have been more than effective.

There was no disputing that Bollow was pretty, though not as attractive as she could have been if she paid more attention to her clothes. She should have worn a skirt instead of jeans and a nice silk blouse—red would go well with her complexion —instead of a striped Indian cotton shirt. And her bag, made of raw leather and sporting, of all things, tassels, had to go. She was in her early thirties and her apparel screamingly exposed her as a warmed-over hippie who had at one time marched against the Vietnam War and American imperialism, venerated Mao Tsetung, carried a copy of his little red book, and hoped to bring socialism to, of all places, staid and stolid Germany, a country with far too few poets and thinkers and far too many philistines and Nazis (whether ex or extant) ever to be able to make that great leap forward to which her disheveled ilk aspired. Somehow, perhaps when she had turned thirty and realized that life was more complicated than her teenage illusions had imagined, she jumped ship and joined the opposition to the left. But her left-wing habits had remained.

We don't change, Romanoff thought. We never change, except perhaps at the edges, where our vision and comprehension are weakest. But our essence—who we are—remains exactly the same, no matter what our age, no matter what our experiences. It was here in Berlin that he had crossed the line of demarcation between the Soviet and American zones and defected. He had been a boy then, of seventeen or eighteen, and now, thirty-odd years later, he was, upon reflection, the same timorous boy who had collected his essentials into a battered leather bag, affected what he hoped would appear as supreme self-confidence, and strolled casually past the sentries, hoping against hope that they wouldn't ask for his papers. Thirty years later, many books and laurels later, he was still a terrified boy caught in the grasp of developments beyond his control. A few weeks ago, life was normal. Now, it was a *bardak*—a mess. How could that possibly have happened?

*

He had joined the glorious Red Army in mid-1944. He was under age, but no one cared. They were hoping to replenish their horrific losses and were willing to accept anyone able to carry a rifle and a knapsack. They gave him the gun, cut his hair, provided some rudimentary instruction on how to fire the damned thing and throw a grenade, and then sent him to the front in Western Ukraine, to an area just east of the city of Lvov, which the Ukrainians absurdly called Lviv. Though on the run, the Germans were still putting up a good fight, but the real danger came from the least expected quarter—the local peasantry. The population greeted the Soviet army sullenly, while the nationalists—their sons and daughters—staged ambushes, sniper shootings, and occasional frontal attacks. We beat them back, usually with high losses, but the perpetual sense of danger lurking behind every bush was nerve-wracking and demoralizing. These headstrong people didn't want to be liberated, so we had no choice but to liberate them against their will.

Barbarism was inevitable, because it wasn't just the nationalists who had to be defeated. The population had to be pacified—taught a lesson about the inevitability and progressiveness of Soviet power. The soldiers surrounded particularly recalcitrant villages suspected of serving as hideouts for the guerrillas and ransacked every house and barn and shed, shooting whoever protested, setting haystacks afire, pouring kerosene into wells, and arresting the young men. He recalled killing two young women, more like girls actually, and an old man in one such village. The women had screamed like banshees and thrown themselves against him, pummeling him with their surprisingly large peasant fists and trying to bite his nose and ears. He pushed them off and, when, like mad bulls, they charged again, he had no choice but to aim his gun at their chests and pull the trigger. The old man, presumably their father, had then charged him, an axe raised above his head. Once again, he had no choice but to shoot and watch his body crumple just short of his feet.

Then there was the mass execution of the thirty or forty nationalists captured after a lengthy firefight during which two of his closest comrades, Borya and Ilya, and a dozen others had lost their lives. They lined them up at the edge of a small clearing—he recalled that the birds had resumed their chirping —and calmly placed a bullet in the back of each man's head. He had pulled the trigger—eagerly, gladly, and vengefully—and watched the brains explode some five or six times, having lost count after the first two. They left the bodies to rot, as reminders to the locals that Soviet power was implacable. It took the recalcitrant Ukrainians some ten years and hundreds of thousands of casualties finally to learn that lesson and abandon the armed struggle.

A few months later Romanoff was encamped on the Vistula River, listening to the daily gunfire and incessant bombardments on the other side, in Warsaw, where the Polish Home Army had staged an uprising in the hope of driving out the Germans, capturing their capital city, and confronting the advancing Soviet army with a *fait accompli*. They had hoped that we would eventually intervene, but, wisely, we didn't. Instead, we waited for the Germans to destroy the stubborn Poles and raze the city. Then we crossed the river and liberated the rubble. Polish corpses, dead men, dead women, dead children, their legs, arms, and heads splayed at odd angles to one another, littered the streets, sidewalks, and trenches. They even clogged the gutters and the sewers, where the nationalists had sought refuge. He recalled the thick stench, the impossibility of sidestepping the bodies, the softness of the flesh beneath his boots, the glint of cracked spectacles, golden teeth, and listless eyeballs. They should have known better than to question the Generalissimo's wisdom.

That's when the worst of the fighting began, in the seven months between Warsaw's liberation and Berlin's occupation. The Germans had become desperate, calling up boys even younger than he was and knowing that, barring the sudden appearance of the miracle weapon that Goebbels promised was being developed, this was their last stand. Desperate men fight desperately, knowing they have nothing to lose and willing to take inordinate risks. We had to fight for every centimeter and we couldn't trust anyone, certainly not the German population that had supported Hitler for so many years or the peoples —Poles, Sorbs, Czechs—who had suffered under the Nazi yoke. They were fair-weather friends who would stab you the moment you turned your back.

Those few months in western Poland and Germany had melded into one indefinable memory, into a protracted migraine, dream, and nightmare. When Romanoff's mind's eye conjured up those days, he heard the explosions—of artillery, guns, bazookas, tanks, and bombs; he heard the cries—of soldiers, children, old men, and women; he smelled the blood, the burnt flesh of humans and animals, the soot and ash that cloaked everything, even the leaves; he tasted the bitter tea, the vile tobacco, and the air that was suffused with human particles and feces; he felt the sliminess of exploded entrails, the stickiness of the wounds, the dirt between his toes, under his arms, and in his ears. All his senses were curiously alive in those days, but it was impossible for him to say with any certainty just where things began, how they developed, and when and where they ended.

The executions, the body pits became a matter of routine, initially worthy of some attention and trepidation, eventually becoming an integral part of one's very being, like an ingrown toenail or a painful tooth. The rapes, which began in the German-populated territories of Poland and the Baltic states, also became routine, almost natural. The women were no less the enemy than the men. They were no less fanatical in their support of Hitler and they were no less likely to fire a gun or cut you up with a knife. He had been shocked the first time he had seen his comrades throw a young girl to the ground. This was madness, he felt, this was vile. This was a violation of everything communism stood for. He had even protested, trying to convince his comrades to desist, to act as human beings, and not as beasts. But we are beasts! one of them had cried. They, the Germans—*she*, he said pointing at the supine girl—made us into beasts. What could he say in response? He turned away in shame, but whether at them or at himself he wasn't sure. The next time the gang rapes occurred, he felt neither shock nor shame nor remorse. Was he an onlooker or a participant? He remembered only the screams, the shouts, and the sweat that poured down his brow. Was he an onlooker or a participant? Were the rapes a nightmare or the reality? Had he dreamed of the quivering thighs, the stench of unwashed genitalia, and his own failures—his own *repeated* failures? Were the rapes a nightmare or were they the reality? And were they his comrades' reality or were they his reality?

And then, suddenly and almost unexpectedly, they were in Berlin and the war—the shooting, the killing, the bloodletting—that had seemed destined to go on endlessly was over. The Germans had capitulated unconditionally, the men were surrendering in droves, and his overworked senses acquired a much-needed respite. The war had stopped and life had returned to something approximating normalcy. Except for the rapes. They continued unabated; indeed, they picked up in intensity and, suddenly and almost unexpectedly, Berlin had become the site of a huge orgy. The Soviet officers winked, turned their heads away, or, more often than not, encouraged the grunts to have some fun—and to take revenge. Here was our chance to get even. The Nazis had raped our land and our women; we would pay them back in kind—severalfold. The German men did nothing and, ashamed of their impotence, crawled into their holes and waited for the Russian fury to run its course. Rape became normal and the women—all women, both young and old—became fair game. Gang rapes became the preferred mode and the only way the German *Fräulein* and *Frauen* could escape the wrath of the victorious Red Army was to become the mistresses of well-heeled officers who offered them protection in exchange for their services. Apparently, some of the Russians had even fallen in love with their prisoners.

Had he taken part? He didn't think so, but, truth to tell, he couldn't be sure. The shock, the ruins, the pervasive smell of death, his youth, his complete lack of experience with women, his mental and physical exhaustion, his inability to perform like a true man, a *muzhik*—all militated against his having been complicit in the rapes. Was it possible that he took part? Everything was possible, but he was sure—well, almost sure—that he was, almost definitely, innocent of the charges levied against him by the five women. It was possible that his inability to remember was the product of the trauma he experienced as a result of the rapes. But, then again, it was far more likely that his memory lapse was due to the overall trauma of the war. Or had he taken part in the rapes?

He *had* killed. He had committed war crimes. He would never be accused of them, because there was no one to launch the accusations. He was certain that no one would even want to make such charges, especially as all sides to the war—the Germans, Russians, Americans, British, and French—had acted with equal, or more or less equal, barbarity. But how did one distinguish slightly more barbarous behavior from slightly less? The world pretended to care about dead Jews, but who cared about dead—or living—Russians? No one. Who cared about dead Ukrainians? Who cared about dead Poles? And who dared to care about dead Germans? In the hecatombs of the war a few women or a few men did not matter and, notwithstanding protestations to the contrary, everyone knew that.

Straight ahead was the Bahnhof Zoo station. If he kept on walking, he'd eventually reach the blackened Reichstag building and the Brandenburg Gate. It was there, before the Wall went up, that he had crossed over into the West. His hotel, was two blocks to his right, on the fashionable Kurfürstendamm. It was still early; the cafés had only just begun to raise their shutters and open their doors. He had time to go to the Wall and saunter amid the wreckage of the past a bit more.

*

As fate, or luck, would have it, Serge Romanoff's childhood had coincided with Stalin's consolidation of power, destruction of counterrevolutionaries and enemy classes, and the grand and glorious revolution from above that propelled Russia and its vassals from the seventeenth into the twentieth century in less than a decade. Millions of Soviet men and women, workers and peasants, young and old had been mobilized for the great cause of socialist construction in the 1930s. His parents had joined enthusiastically. His father, Ivan, who hailed from a muddy village in the Middle Volga region, had fought in the Revolution on the side of the Bolsheviks because they promised the poorest peasants like himself land; he had been among the first in his village to welcome collectivization; and then, when the opportunity arose to acquire an accelerated education as an engineer in Moscow—the capital, the light of the revolution, the beacon of world communism—he had leapt at the chance. Although his surname raised some eyebrows, his Party credentials were impeccable; he had distinguished himself in the struggle against the kulaks, the rich peasants who throttled the village poor and resisted the imposition of Soviet power. It was in Moscow, in the engineering institute, that he had met and, being a true believer in a hurry, married Romanoff's mother, Maria, within days of their first encounter at a Party meeting, where they chanced to be sitting next to each other in the front row. She, too, had come to the big city from some godforsaken village several hundred miles southeast of the capital and, like Ivan, had been an enthusiastic Bolshevik since late 1917 when she first joined a band of deserters in pillaging the local nobleman's estate. Sergei Ivanovich Romanov, the future historian who would drop the *i* in his first name and replace the *v* with a double-*f* in his surname on the grounds that, as he put it, the new spelling conjured up images of Montmartre and not horse manure and hay, was born in 1930.

The young family lived in a *kommunalka*, a communal apartment that formerly belonged to some fat capitalist, but that now was shared by as many, if not more, deserving families as there were rooms. The women took turns cooking in the roach-infested kitchen and everyone took turns in the unventilated bathroom and malodorous toilet. Their room was small, probably having belonged to a harshly exploited servant girl, but it had the distinct advantage of being exclusively theirs. Other families had to inhabit the same large room divided by a thin curtain. Both lovemaking and fighting became public events under such crowded conditions. The adults complained about the stench emanating from the toilet and the smell of fried lard that permeated all the rooms, but the children enjoyed the proximity of so many friends.

Both parents were active Party members, attending all

the meetings, listening attentively to endless reports, avidly reading Party newspapers, and marching in all the parades. They were, they told young Serge, building a new civilization, one that would surpass in achievement and wealth every society that had formerly existed on the face of the earth. And the man leading the struggle for the new civilization was the great Joseph Stalin, the avuncular, mustachioed figure with a wise, omniscient smile and crisp white uniform depicted on the posters that hid the peeling wallpaper on their walls. He cared for every little boy and girl, for every man and woman, for every peasant and worker. But he brooked no opposition from the bourgeoisie, kulaks, priests, and other capitalist scum. Those he stamped out like the vermin they were.

In 1937, Serge asked his parents why several of the families living in the *kommunalka* had left the lodgings without so much as saying good-bye. His father replied unflinchingly, "They had been exposed as enemies of the people." His mother then added, "And do you know what happens to enemies of the people, Seryozha?" He reflected for a moment and then happily answered, "They're shot or sent to Siberia!" He had no notion of what it meant to be shot and Siberia could have been anywhere, but he understood that that was the wise Stalin's way of caring for his people. It was that year, on May Day, that he first joined his parents in a parade. Papa carried him on his shoulders and he waved a little red flag and marveled at the sea of well-wishers who had come to show their love of the great leader—the *vozhd*.

He vaguely recalled the trials of Bukharin and other Japanese and Polish spies. At school, the teacher discussed their cases in great detail, explaining just how these so-called Bolsheviks had managed to conceal their illicit, treasonous doings for so many years. We are, she intoned—her face coming to resemble Lenin's, when he rallied the working class in defense of the revolution in 1918—surrounded by capitalist and imperialist enemies who detest the Soviet people and, most of all, Comrade Stalin. In order to undermine our achievements, they worm their way into our social fabric—it had occurred to Serge at that moment that Bukharin really did resemble a worm—and attempt to sabotage our economy and divide our Party. But Stalin didn't let them! Neither did the Soviet people, who were always vigilant, always watchful for the slimy, traitorous snakes who slithered on their bellies before the almighty dollar. Serge decided that he would, when grown up, join the ranks of the Chekists, the noble organization established by Iron Feliks Dzerzhinsky that dedicated itself to unswerving loyalty and unconditional defense of the Soviet Motherland.

Membership in the Pioneers followed and, after that, when he was already a teenager, came the Komsomol—the Young Leninist League, the anteroom to membership in the Communist Party of the Soviet Union. Young Serge discovered he had a remarkable talent for foreign languages, learning Bulgarian, Polish, and Finnish while still in middle school. His future, as a distinguished member of Stalin's phalanx of loyal linguists, seemed assured. But there was no time to bask in one's future laurels. War came, just as Stalin had predicted, in the form of fascist Germany's dastardly stab in the back. His father immediately volunteered and, hoping to defend Moscow against the fascist hordes, stepped on a Soviet mine and was blown to bits on the very first day he saw action. His aggrieved mother joined the women in digging trenches and building tank traps. It was inevitable that, when he came of age or, more precisely, looked to be of age, the future Serge Ivanovich Romanoff would follow in their footsteps and do his Bolshevik duty. He joined the army willingly, enthusiastically. His homeland was under assault by German barbarians. The wise and brilliant Simonov had taught that every Russian had a sacred obligation to kill Germans. Serge decided he would take great pleasure in doing just that.

The reality proved to be more complicated. Shooting at a distance was one thing. Firing a bullet into a defenseless man's skull was another. Doing that scores of times was still another. By the time he reached Berlin, Romanoff's communist ardor had dimmed. He still believed in the cause, but, after having witnessed, and brought about, so much death and devastation, he was no longer absolutely sure that the cause made sense—or, at the very least, that his involvement in the cause made sense. Stalin was wise, Stalin was great, *da, da, da*—but the blood on his hands was a constant reminder of his own frailty, mortality, and complicity in—there was no other word for it—evil. The construction of communism justified such evil—and that assuaged Serge's aching conscience somewhat—but, even so, evil remained evil. He would have preferred to have built communism only with good—that is to say, communist—means, but his experience in the war suggested that was impossible. Could he live with so much blood on his hands? He would have to.

His tortured ruminations had ended and Romanoff glanced up from the sidewalk. There it was—the place where he had met his destiny. Romanoff had reached the Brandenburg Gate and the Wall.

*

A few years after he crossed over to West Berlin, Romanoff was persuaded by some correspondent from Radio Liberty—a greasy man who spoke an archaic Russian and openly declared that he was a member of the rightwing People's Labor Union, which, he insisted, would one day topple the Communist regime —to pen an essay about his escape. Romanoff had some qualms, but finally agreed, figuring that a little bit of publicity couldn't hurt his efforts to establish himself in the West. He entitled it "I, too, chose freedom," playing off the bestselling memoir, *I Chose Freedom*, of Viktor Kravchenko, a high-ranking Ukrainian Communist who had defected in Washington just after the war. Kravchenko's book had caused a splash, exposing Stalin and his system as inhuman, and gotten him into serious trouble with the Soviet secret police, the NKVD, which regarded assassination as the only suitable way of dealing with treasonous émigrés. Romanoff's carefully crafted account eschewed criticism of the USSR and simply told the story of his escape—but without providing any of the background. And that, of course, was the best part of the story.

A colonel of the secret police, one Aleksei Mamontov, had befriended him in an East Berlin tavern frequented by Soviet military personnel. Their first meeting appeared to have been serendipitous, or so Serge initially believed, as it was Romanoff who had asked Mamontov if he could park himself at his table and not the other way around. Were this an NKVD operation, Romanoff not unreasonably supposed, Mamontov would have taken the initiative. Romanoff developed an immediate liking for the stocky, thick-necked, fat-lipped, bald, and bespectacled Russian who almost resembled a caricature of a Soviet commissar. Mamontov had a taste for the sardonic and the ironic, qualities in short supply among most Communists, and, like Romanoff, was well read, preferring Shakespeare to the Russian classics and considering the tenets of socialist realism to be appropriate only at the earliest stages of socialist construction—in the Soviet case, in the 1930s, and not after the war. These ideas, hinting at heretofore unimagined vistas for communism's future, were new and exciting to Romanoff, who had never encountered such lack of orthodoxy among his parents, school friends, or army buddies.

They would meet regularly, on Fridays, and, besides conducting lofty conversations about the arts—it was, frankly, Mamontov who did most of the talking—would also bemoan the barracks cooking, the ugliness of the East German girls, and the chaotic administration in the city. Mamontov revealed that he had been posted to eastern Poland after its Belorussian and Ukrainian peasants and workers had been liberated by the Soviet regime in September 1939, and Romanoff, struck by the coincidence, related his own misadventures in Lvov province in 1944. His voice lowered, Mamontov then confided that his duties involved hunting down bourgeois nationalists and that the highpoint of his stay in that region came just after Hitler betrayed Stalin and attacked the USSR on June 22, 1941. Some twenty or thirty thousand Ukrainian, Polish, and Jewish political prisoners had to be liquidated, an operation Mamontov oversaw in one of western Ukraine's larger towns. They used machine guns and grenades and threw the corpses into deep pits, where they rotted in the summer heat, producing, he was later informed, an impossible stench. "This was class struggle at its best—and bloodiest," he observed dryly. Mamontov appeared shaken as he spoke and Serge, impressed by his openness and sincerity, confided that he, too, had killed nationalists with brutal means.

"They never learn," Mamontov remarked sadly.

"A tragedy," Romanoff replied.

"And such a waste, such a terrible, terrible waste."

One day, Mamontov informed Serge that the secret police were looking into his dossier. Romanoff was stunned. He and his parents had been model Communists. His record in the army had been spotless. Mamontov filled his glass and Serge downed a large vodka to steady his nerves. Apparently, there had been a denunciation by one of the residents of the *kommunalka*—something about insufficient vigilance by his mother in the face of imperialist provocations. The NKVD had no choice but to investigate and who knew where that would lead, especially for Serge. Fortunately, there was a simple way for Serge to set things right. He should go west and serve Russia there. At some future point, he could return or—who knows?—possibly even stay and continue to help the Soviet Motherland in his newfound capacity—perhaps as a writer, perhaps as a journalist, perhaps as a professor. Romanoff knew he had no choice but to agree.

Mamontov even helped with the cross-over. He met Serge at the gate of his barracks and handed him a pigskin case with some documents that, he assured him, would be of interest to the officials in West Berlin. I am not a traitor, Romanoff, ashen and nervous, weakly protested, but Mamontov reassured him that they were innocuous papers dealing with logistics in his compound. It was nothing of any value to anybody, but it would serve to establish his credentials in the West.

"You need a cover, my young friend," Mamontov stated, hoping that his solicitude would have a calming effect on the young man. "We need you to be in America, to become a loyal American." Romanoff's brow darkened and Mamontov corrected himself: "To *seem* to be a loyal American, while always serving the Soviet Motherland. Don't worry, my young friend. We shall never leave you alone." Romanoff couldn't fathom whether Mamontov's last sentence was a promise or a threat, but he knew he had no choice but to take the documents and promise to do his best.

"We know you will," Mamontov gently assured him. "You are among the chosen," he added mysteriously and let go of Romanoff's hand.

After Romanoff changed into oversized civilian clothes in a nearby pub, the two of them boarded the S-Bahn, disembarked at Friedrichstrasse, and strolled along the Unter den Linden boulevard toward the Brandenburg Gate. Most of the linden trees had been chopped down or ravaged during the fighting; the buildings on both sides of the avenue still displayed bullet holes and sizable cracks, some running along their entire facades; and the rubble remained piled high. But the red flag hung proudly from the Soviet Embassy, street cars crisscrossed the thoroughfare, and a few cafés appeared to have returned to life.

According to the version in "I, too, chose freedom," Romanoff crossed into West Berlin on his own, his heart pounding madly and his hopes of a new life in a new world rising with every tremulous step he took. In reality, Mamontov accompanied him to the very line of demarcation and, when the guards were busy examining some cyclist with a suspiciously large package, pushed him across and whispered, "*Do svidaniia.*" Romanoff lost his balance, wheeled around, found his footing, and muttered good-bye. Upon catching sight of the ridiculously awkward boy in a faded brown suit that must have once belonged to a much heftier uncle, the Americans broke into laughter and slapped him on the back. For the second time in under a minute, Romanoff almost fell. His arrival in the West had not begun propitiously.

His West German hosts weren't terribly impressed by the documents Mamontov had given him, but they took them as evidence of Romanoff's good will. A slim American with a crew cut, who informed Romanoff that he was sacrificing his college football career at Alabama by serving in the army, subjected him to a lackadaisical interview in his accented Russian. Serge claimed to have defected because he wanted to be free of the shackles of Stalinism. That bit hurt, as nothing could have been further from the truth, but Romanoff followed Mamontov's orders to the letter, suspecting that any deviation would get him into hot water with both sides, a fate he did not envy. The Americans let him go, the West Germans gave him lice-infested lodging and a small stipend, and he spent the next few years learning the ways of the capitalist West, doing odd jobs, and learning a variety of old Slavic, Turkic, and Norse languages—"for the hell of it," as he later put it.

"We are certain," Mamontov had once stated without specifying just who *we* were, "that, if you apply yourself, you can become one of the world's greatest historians."

"Me?" Romanoff had replied in disbelief. "I know nothing about history."

"You will learn," Mamontov had declared peremptorily. "We will help you."

Once again, the *we* was unspecified—although Romanoff naturally assumed it referred to the NKVD—and the help was left undefined. It materialized every few months in the form of letters posted in various West German cities containing several hundred dollars—an enormous amount of money in those days—and a note (presumably from Mamontov) reminding him to avoid ostentatious displays of suddenly acquired wealth and to save the money for a later day. Romanoff had some qualms about taking capitalist currency, but, once again, there was no reasonable alternative. He realized one day, while sipping a coffee at Kranzler's, on the Ku'damm, that he had stepped onto the slippery slope and was rapidly becoming a full-time employee of the Soviet secret police. So be it, he decided. There are far worse fates than helping the Chekists guard socialism from imperialist assaults.

Did the Soviet secret police smooth Romanoff's way to America? Did they help him get accepted for studies at Harvard? Possibly, though he believed he had achieved both goals on his own. In all likelihood, the NKVD's assistance came later, when Romanoff was working on his treatise on Rasha's origins and development. His American colleagues insisted that, as a deserter, he'd never get a visa to do research in the Soviet archives. But he did—and not just once, but every time he applied. Since the applications were all vetted by the secret police, Romanoff knew that his guardian angel in the NKVD had to be acting on his behalf. Moreover, whether in Moscow, Leningrad, or Kiev, Romanoff never had any difficulties getting complete and immediate access to whichever archives he desired to see. The archivists even offered to make complimentary photostats of the materials he requested. Though not too much at once, please, they pleaded, as our technical base is a bit out of date.

He met Mamontov, visibly aged and grown even more rotund, on these trips, usually in one of the few restaurants that had more or less full menus and therefore catered to foreigners. "There's no reason for us to hide in shadows, my young friend," he reassured Romanoff. "We are old friends and old friends have the right to drink vodka and laugh in public, do they not?" Only occasionally did Mamontov ask him about his life in Cambridge. And he never questioned him about his research. Instead, they talked of old times, exchanged jokes, and drank—usually three or four bottles, with twice as many beer chasers. Romanoff suspected that his friend's lack of curiosity could probably be explained by his knowing everything about him anyway, but he appreciated his discretion nonetheless—perhaps because it sustained the illusion of his being an independent scholar.

Stalin's death on March 5, 1953 came as a brutal shock to Romanoff, who, like so many of his countrymen, had come to assume that the great leader would live forever. He cried upon hearing the news; his grief was attenuated only by the knowledge that the entire progressive world was grieving with him —from the commonest Russian peasant to such heroic figures as the Negro Communist, Paul Robeson. What followed Stalin's tragic demise was even more disturbing. Misguided East Germans had the temerity to demand the Party's resignation a few months later. Later that year, the head of the Soviet secret police, Lavrentii Beria, was executed by his erstwhile comrades, while his Polish counterpart, Józef Światło, defected. The Chekists sustained communism. If they began leaving, what would remain of the house that Lenin and Stalin built?

Then, in 1956, that upstart Khrushchev dared to denounce Stalin at the Twentieth Party Congress in Moscow. The momentous secret speech he delivered to a select audience was leaked to the Western intelligence services by a Pole (who else?) who wrote an account of his defection entitled "I chose truth"—and then beamed back to Eastern Europe by Radio Free Europe and Radio Liberty. Romanoff had to laugh. The Polish defector's handlers in the CIA were obviously familiar with the "I chose" genre of defector confessions established by Kravchenko and himself. Taking their cue from the portly Party leader, the perpetually dissatisfied Poles took to the streets and the Hungarians tried to roll back socialism with arms. Although he had lived in the West for close to a decade, Romanoff's worlds—the world of his dreams and the world of his hopes—were crumbling before his eyes. Fortunately, Mamontov remained unaffected, assuring him that the difficulties were temporary and imploring him to remember that his pursuit of a successful career was the best way for him to continue supporting the Motherland.

Aleksei died in 1965, probably of natural causes, though Romanoff couldn't be sure, given that his death followed on the heels of Khrushchev's ouster. The effect on Romanoff was almost immediate. Acquiring a visa became slightly more cumbersome. No more letters with money arrived. No one tried to contact him, either in Moscow or Leningrad or in Cambridge. The archivists still served him happily and assiduously, but, overall, he appeared to have fallen off the KGB's radar, perhaps because he had been Mamontov's pet project and, with Aleksei's passing, he no longer had a handler. If so, Romanoff thought, then I am free—not in general (as a loyal Soviet subject, he had always been that), but with respect to the secret police. He had collaborated willingly, if somewhat naively, but it was a relief to know he had no one to report to anymore. To be honest, Romanoff reluctantly admitted to himself, I have lost my former zeal. I still support the socialist cause and I still venerate Stalin, but he's dead and his successors, in both the Soviet Union and the other socialist states, have betrayed his legacy. Mamontov and I may have been the last true believers. Now, he's gone and I am no longer sure what I believe. Fortunately, there were his books and his theory of Rasha. Those were eternal achievements that had helped consolidate socialism in his country. On that score, as on so many others, the good Mamontov had been absolutely right.

*

And here was the Wall. What a portentous symbol of his current predicament! If the scandal surrounding the five women continued, who knew what the repercussions for his career would be. He'd survive, as would his books, but his reputation in America would be stained, at least for a few years. Worse, the affair might draw the attention of the overzealous Soviet secret police, always on the look-out for scandals it could manipulate to its advantage. Some ambitious agent might find his file and decide to renew the connection. That would be an inconvenience, especially in light of his diminished commitment to whatever remained of the Soviet cause under that doddering old fool, Brezhnev.

He clambered up the platform to get a closer look at No Man's Land and the East. Somewhere in that vast expanse was Hitler's bunker. How ironic that it should have survived the end of his mad world in a physical space accessible to no one. It was as if Hitler had been confined, not to hell, but to purgatory or limbo. How appropriate, he decided, recalling his speech on war and violence at the Turkish restaurant. Squinting and craning his neck, Romanoff could identify the exact path he and Mamontov had taken on that fateful day. Now, the line of demarcation was marked by a mammoth concrete barrier, gnarled bunches of barbed wire, forlorn guard towers reminiscent of prisons, and armed soldiers with dogs. Beyond them stood the gray prefabricated buildings assigned to the East German elite. What were they afraid of? Socialism was supposed to be superior to capitalism as both ideology and system. Why not let the capitalists come and see for themselves what they were missing? Why not let your own people convince themselves of the benefits of socialism? It was so sad, the Wall, and so unnecessary. Mamontov had defended it as a desperate measure to save East Germany from imperialism's predations, but Romanoff could see, even then, that his friend wasn't persuaded by his own argument.

Sieglinde Bollow had also spoken of the Wall as an aberration. She had initially supported it, but, then, after finally seeing the light, had come to hate it. Hers was an interesting journey, Romanoff thought, though hardly unique. There were many former socialists who had abandoned their left-wing ideals and found succor among the right, sometimes even the radical right. It was as if their fanatical commitment to one side required that they become as fanatically committed to the other side. There appeared to be no middle ground; they were either on this side of the Wall or on that side. Could he think of any exceptions to this apparent rule? No, he could not, not just yet. And then, as a broad smile crept crab-like across his face, he realized that he was wrong. He was the exception. He had been a fanatical believer in the cause and now—what was he, *exactly*, now? Certainly not a fanatical Communist and certainly not a fanatical capitalist. He was somewhere in between—in No Man's Land. It was, he reflected, a not uncomfortable place to be. He had his books, he had his research, and, when the bullets didn't fly and the screams in his head abated, he could even concentrate on his work.

But first there was Bollow. She was too self-absorbed for his taste, but she appeared to be a good and honest journalist who would want to hear his side of the story. The absurd seduction had prevented him—and her—from pursuing that angle, but it was plainly important for him to meet with her again, before this affair spun completely out of control and as long as there was a chance of containing some of the worst damage. But that would mean telling her about all his wartime experiences. Would she understand? Possibly. Would she forgive him the atrocities he had committed? Or would she decide they proved conclusively that he was both capable of and culpable for the rapes? The dormant left-winger in her would cry for his blood, but the reborn right-winger might appreciate that men and women did things in war that they would never normally do under conditions of peace.

Romanoff turned into the park, intending to wend his way to the hotel via its wooded lanes. Just after war's end, this had been a wasteland of stumped and scarred and leafless trees resembling a witch's hideout. What hadn't been destroyed in the fighting had been plundered by the civilian population to heat their cold stoves. How swiftly, how assuredly, how irreversibly had the master race descended to the level of groveling Russian peasants, willing to trade all their belongings, no matter how deeply sentimental, for a can of smelly sardines. The men, who had strutted along the streets of occupied Europe for five years, now scurried about like emaciated rats, their eyes turned away, their hands dirty, their pants frayed. And the women, even while recovering from the shock of the mass rapes, had taken to the streets, peddling their bodies for cigarettes and coffee, forgetting completely their former claims to be the most beautiful, the most vigorous, the most seductive in all of Europe.

The sun cast dappled shadows through the mostly green leaves. As a yellow leaf fluttered like a butterfly before him, Romanoff espied a thin young boy with upturned eyelashes and a ruby-red mouth gazing at him from behind a tree. The youth grabbed his crotch, thrust it forward, and, his voice a sultry baritone, sang the refrain from Marlene Dietrich's signature song in *The Blue Angel* while grinding his slim hips:

Ich bin vom Kopf bus Fuss

auf Liebe eingestellt,
denn das ist meine Welt
und sonst gar nichts.

Taken aback by this disturbing intrusion, Romanoff mumbled something incoherent and, head bowed, eyes averted, heart thumping, kept on marching—left, right, left, right, left, right, almost as if he were still in the army—and accelerated his pace. As he was almost out of earshot, the boy cried, *"Schade, Liebling, vielleicht ein anderes Mal?"*

He had never heard Marlene assert her commitment to nothing else but love, from head to foot no less, in quite such a context. As he laughed at the boy's disappointment and hope of another time, it suddenly struck Romanoff that the solution to his problems was quite simple. His chance encounter with the effeminate youth had given him the answer to all his difficulties. Sieglinde Bollow had probably wondered why he had failed to respond to her seduction. Chances were she had surmised he was —what was the German word for gay?—*schwul*. German society was still fairly conservative and its attitudes toward gays were mixed. But Berlin had a large gay community in Berlin near Nollendorfplatz. Bollow might disapprove, but she had no choice but to be tolerant or pretend to be tolerant.

What if he went along and confessed to her that he was a closet homosexual—indirectly and by inference, naturally? Several things would follow. Her anxieties about her own charms would be alleviated; her advances would be put to an end; she could not help, being a West German ex-*Revoluzzer* and emancipated woman, or *Emanze*, but sympathize with his plight; and, most important, she would have to come to the irrefutable conclusion that he could not possibly have committed the rapes. It would be easy enough to concoct a story about his early discovery of his proclivities, about his desperate attempts to hide them, about the repressive atmosphere in America, about the lack of understanding shown by his Harvard colleagues. Best of all, there was zero chance of her going public with the revelation, which meant that his life back home, or here in Germany, would remain unaffected. Oddly enough, by confessing to this imagined weakness, Romanoff would be acquiring the upper hand—the position of dominance—in their relations. He could not resist a smirk. Mamontov would be proud of his star pupil's ability to twist reality.

CHAPTER FIVE

News of Romanoff's difficulties came as a godsend to Professor Boris Ivanov of Yale University. He had been reading a dissertation about Peter the Great's barbaric treatment of the rebellious sharpshooters, or *streltsy*, when his graduate research assistant knocked on his door and showed him a copy of *The New York Times*. Had the professor seen the story on page eight? he asked, dropping the newspaper onto Ivanov's oak desk next to the ashtray piled high with cigarette butts. The professor didn't like being disturbed, but his RA guessed correctly that he wouldn't want to pass up the sensational story about his reviled nemesis. After seeing the page-five headline—"Harvard Professor Accused of Rape in Berlin"—Ivanov lit his pipe, settled into his easy chair, and readied himself for a pleasant read.

The fifty-five-year old chairman of the history department and author of several important monographs on early Slavic history had been Romanoff's main detractor for close to twenty years. According to his official biography, Ivanov's parents, both ardent supporters of the *ancien régime* toppled by the Bolsheviks, had fled to the Crimea in 1919 following General Denikin's unfortunate defeat, boarded an overcrowded steamer that almost capsized in the strong currents of the Bosporus before finally docking in Constantinople—then the object of contention among the British, French, Italians, and Turks—and, after his mother peddled all her jewelry to some unscrupulous merchant in the Grand Bazaar, continued in a rat-infested tub to Marseilles, whence they finally reached Paris, the prized destination of many White Russians escaping Lenin's soldiers, mobs, and executioners.

After Ivanov was born in 1920, his parents decided to make their way for the land of boundless opportunity; fortunately for them, they managed to emigrate to New York just before the United States closed its borders to immigrants in 1924. The father worked as a security guard on Wall Street; the mother cleaned offices on Union Square. But they made ends meet, while living on Fourteenth Street, in the slums that bordered on the muck-filled East River, among the many other Slavic émigrés, and attending the Divine Liturgy at the Russian church on East First. Young Boris entered the elite Stuyvesant High School, received straight A's, and applied to Yale, which endowed him with a full four-year scholarship. He went on to complete his Ph.D., writing a brilliant dissertation on the Norse influence on medieval Novgorod.

Ivanov was certain that Romanoff, his main competitor in the world of Russian historians, was a charlatan. He railed against him and his theories in his books, in his articles, and in his conference presentations, but, for reasons that he could not fathom, the force of his arguments had little to no impact on scholarly views. Romanoff was the *Wunderkind*, the *enfant terrible*, the boy genius, while he was simply a competent scholar who spent too much time quibbling over details that didn't fit his own preconceptions of what Russian, and more generally Slavic, history was. Ivanov knew how and why academic fashions came and went. Scholars wanted the Cold War to be over and therefore welcomed anybody who claimed that Russia was an ancient civilization that long predated today's ephemeral conflicts between East and West. It also helped that Romanoff was genuinely handsome, while he was a caricature of the absent-minded, badly shaved, and poorly clad professor. Images were more potent than reality and, when it came to image, Romanoff beat him hands down.

But not when it came to the substance of their scholarship, or so Ivanov insisted. There were three fatal problems with Romanoff's work. The first was painfully obvious to any objectively inclined expert: he was wrong about the origins of Rasha and its supposedly ancient civilization. There was a case to be made for Russia's origins in the Khazar polity that emerged between the Black and Caspian Seas sometime in the sixth century; despite the contrarian views of Ukrainian and Belorussian nationalists, there was also a case to be made for Russia's origins in the Kievan state that took root on the Dnieper in the ninth. Sadly, history had been unkind to Russia and the Mongol invasion in the thirteenth century interrupted our history until, some two hundred years later, proud Muscovy cast off the yoke and assumed the mantle of Kiev, which was, is, and would always remain the Mother of Russian cities. In either case, the notion that something called Rah-shah—a preposterous term, conjuring up cheerleaders and Iranian potentates!—could have existed in the Dnieper-Volga area as early as the fifth century was absolute nonsense, balderdash of the kind that only ignorant freshmen could possibly concoct. Professor Ivanov snickered, as he was momentarily reminded of an ignorant undergraduate who had once written that the founder of the Cheka had been Chekhov! The stupid boy had failed the exam and the course and soon changed his major from history to English.

The sheer stupidity of Romanoff's views led to the second problem. In advancing a transparently wrong version of Russia's origins, Romanoff was effectively providing ideological ammunition to the ignorant non-Russian historians who disputed Russia's organic connection to Kiev. These historical illiterates ranged from Polish and Lithuanian chauvinists who hoped to recreate the Polish-Lithuanian Commonwealth to White Russians who insisted that the language of Kiev was, of all things, Belorussian to Little Russians—excuse me, Ukrainians!—who had the nerve to claim that Russia didn't come into existence until Peter the Great renamed Muscovy in the early eighteenth century. If Romanoff was the best Russia could produce, then all these irksome nationalities would have a clear field for their erroneous theories.

The third problem with Romanoff's work was equally

obvious to anyone who cared to go to the archives and examine the rare documents Romanoff claimed to have unearthed: either they did not exist or they were fabrications. That was the only explanation Ivanov could think of for the complete lack of cooperation the sullen Russian archivists who had so worshipfully serviced Romanoff evinced when he asked to see the same materials. He had even brought copies of Romanoff's books and pointed to the relevant footnotes. *Nyet*, they had replied stonily, we cannot help you. Why not? he had demanded. At which point, they had turned away, but not before requesting that he be attentive to the other researchers and preserve the decorum of the archive.

He had tried several times and each time the answer had been the same. He had even asked his graduate assistants to take a shot. They, too, had received no cooperation, even after offering liquor, cigarettes, nylons, copies of *Playboy* magazine, or outright money. The archivists were unmovable in their dedication to communist rectitude. Romanoff was their favorite, which also meant that he had to be the Party's—as well as the secret police's—favorite. But why hide such important documents from other researchers? If they were genuine, their broad dissemination could only advance scholarship, promote Russian identity, and serve the Soviet cause of rapprochement with the West. It made no sense, Ivanov concluded. The only thing that did make sense was that the documents were forgeries and that Romanoff either knew, in which case he was a scoundrel, or did not, in which case he was a dupe. Either way, the man deserved to be dethroned from his position as tsar of Russian studies in America and banished to the functional equivalent of Siberia— some community college in Idaho.

Unfortunately, the field was and had always been a haven for Russian mountebanks. If they supported the tsarist or Soviet regimes, they tended to be cheap propagandists. If they were opponents, they bore the grudges that all losers always bear. Both groups placed ideology above integrity and produced screeds that passed for scholarship only because the Americans themselves were too inexperienced, too ignorant, too naïve, too, well, stupid to understand that no Russian could possibly be objective about Russia in the twentieth century. When his interlocutors responded to this broadside by asking him whether he was the exception to the rule, and why, he would always answer with a spry rebuttal that shut them up. In point of fact, he was a Baltic German. The family had exchanged Müller for an anodyne Russian surname to escape persecution during the Revolution and Civil War, when any kind of suspicious affiliation—with priests, bourgeois intellectuals, or untrustworthy nationalities—could get you shot. The story, besides evoking sympathy and silencing would-be critics, also had the virtue of being true. Which was far more than he could say about the charlatans.

One group of losers were especially annoying: those who came to hate and oppose the Soviets after having been their enthusiastic supporters and willing collaborators. Trotsky was a perfect example. The man had been a savage, murdering hundreds of thousands of innocent peasants, workers, and bourgeois. He had been no less ruthless than Lenin and Stalin and was up to his neck in blood. Once in the West, however, he changed his spots and rechristened himself as a democrat who opposed Stalin. Now there was the dialectic at work! And the West—what did the West do? It welcomed him as if he were a morally spotless saint. His fortuitous assassination in Mexico sealed the case for his sainthood. Too bad he hadn't lived to witness the Second World War. What would he have done when Stalin and Hitler signed a non-aggression pact in 1939? Would he have supported Uncle Joe after Germany turned on the USSR in 1941? What a pleasure it would have been to see him and his many reverent underlings at American universities squirm.

Romanoff had to go, so much was clear to Ivanov. The Americans were too blinded by his good looks to realize the depth of the deception that he, and his Soviet handlers, had foisted upon the scholarly world. But they were also too moralistic to ignore the charges that had been levelled against him by the women. One rape might have been ignored as hearsay, but five! Five were solid evidence of wrongdoing and moral turpitude even if one or two of the women were mistaken. A petition! That's what he would do. Organize a petition for Romanoff's temporary suspension from his academic duties. If enough scholars signed, Harvard's president might just feel impelled to quash a possible scandal by caving to the petition's demands.

Unfortunately for Professor Ivanov, the petition proved to be a bust. Most of his colleagues insisted they couldn't believe the allegations were true. After all, Romanoff was known for his impeccable character and moral backbone. So why dispute something that was obviously false? Others said they were worried by the allegations—who wouldn't be?—but preferred not to take a public stand—well, not just yet. Perhaps when the evidence was conclusive. A few insisted the charges had to be a KGB plot intended to destroy the career of this generation's best Russian historian. *That*, Ivanov thought bitterly, was a transparent jibe against him, a crude and uncalled-for low blow. After some ten phone calls, his afternoon wasted on the futile pursuit of academics with a moral backbone, Ivanov slammed the phone into the receiver, lit a cigarette, sat back in the leathery folds of his chair, and, with thoughts of vengeance circulating in his head, cursed his colleagues for their cowardice and stupidity. Someday, yes, someday, they would come around. Should he be magnanimous or should he turn his gaze away from their pathetic pleas for forgiveness?

It was, he eventually decided, time to consider more extreme measures. A former student, John Buckley—a Greenwich, Connecticut WASP who sported lime-green Polo shirts on his days off and loved to sail (preferably in the Long Island Sound, though the Wannsee would do), but was no relation of the conservative pundit—had written a fine dissertation about Soviet historians and their views on Russian state building, but, unable to land a decent academic job on one of the coasts, had found employment as an analyst with the Central Intelligence Agency and was apparently based in Berlin. Ivanov had no idea what his job entailed, but he assumed it would have something to do with

Russia. Buckley might just be interested in hearing his former professor's views of a man who was sullying the profession and possibly collaborating with the Soviets. Ivanov's yellow teeth shone briefly as he curled his lips. Wouldn't it be ironic if the CIA decided to use the scandal to recruit Romanoff? I would know and he would know that I know and that would be the end of his prepossessing behavior—at least toward me.

And then there was another possibility. Professor Vyacheslav Skriabin of Moscow State University, a friend and a colleague who also specialized in early Russian history and considered Romanoff's ideas to be bunk, might be mobilized to take action at his end. Skriabin would be reluctant to take on the rape charge, as it placed Russia in a bad light, but he might be willing to use the scandal as a means of undermining Romanoff's credibility in the Soviet Union—both in the archives that were so accommodating and—why not?—the KGB. This could get tricky, Ivanov concluded, rubbing out the cigarette and lighting another one, but there was enough distance between the Lubyanka and Yale to make him immune to just about any kind of blow-up in Moscow or Berlin.

*

Surprised that he wasn't the abject supplicant with hat in hand, his usual role in his relations with Ivanov, Buckley reacted to the professor's phone call with unrepressed delight. Yes, he had heard of Romanoff. Who hadn't? And yes, he was working on Russia, though strictly analytical work, "no cloak and dagger stuff." Had he heard about the scandal? No, not really, he answered, what scandal? The five rape charges, Ivanov said. In Berlin—your town. In his excitement at finally getting someone to listen to his complaints, the professor's voice had acquired a staccato quality.

"Five women. Germans, all German. Charges of rape. Yes, rape. After the war. Yes, in Berlin, your town. Berlin! Yes, Berlin! When the Russians came. The wave of rapes, yes, the wave of rapes. Maybe a million, maybe more, maybe two million. And five of these women, yes, five, all from Berlin. Five of them made charges. Against that Romanoff. Yes, against Romanoff—Serge Ivanovich Romanoff. They said"—he took several quick breaths —"that Serge Ivanovich Romanoff had raped them. Hah!" Out of breath once again and uncertain of what more to say, Ivanov ended with "and that's that." Then he added, "I figured you might be interested. This is your field, yes?"

Buckley was interested, obviously. Any scandal involving Russian émigrés and their shadowy world's endless intrigues, back-stabbings, and conspiracies could shed light on their entanglements vis-à-vis the Soviet Union and, thus, on the inscrutable workings of its security services. This tidbit was particularly juicy and the ambitious Buckley was miffed by his having missed it. He was supposed to know these things. After all, an Ivy League Ph.D. opened doors to the Agency, but it did little to sustain or augment one's standing once you were inside. The much-vaunted old boys' network that supposedly guaranteed advancement was far less effective than its female detractors made it out to be. This was espionage and, while incompetents were promoted even in the best of organizations, the Agency had to take special care to keep them as far down the ladder as possible. Lives were always on the line and he had to produce results, his boss never failed to remind him, without ever quite clarifying what those results were. Buckley was expected to keep abreast of events in the Soviet Union and keep an eye on Soviet activities in East Berlin. If possible, his youthful appearance, easy charm, knowledge of literary Russian, and decent German —good enough to enable him to carry on a conversation, but flawed enough to disarm his interlocutors and lower their guard —were to translate into the recruitment of confidential informers who wouldn't mind having a beer and sharing their views of what German students, especially on the left, were up to.

True or not, Romanoff's possible connection to the Soviets made him vulnerable, both to the CIA and the KGB. It was too late to blackmail him: the cat had gotten out of the bag. But we could offer to kill the news about the rapes and defuse the situation as soon and as much as possible. Romanoff would be grateful and both of us would know that he was now on our hook, owing us a favor—or possibly two or three. Since the KGB, which had its own agents of influence in West Germany's power structures, would be up to the same tricks as the CIA, it was therefore a question of who could get to Romanoff first. He'd presumably be more inclined to treat us more favorably—after all, the United States was his home—but one never knew with these hotshot Russians. He might decide to play a double game.

"Thank you, Professor Ivanov," Buckley declared and hung up. That felt especially good, to be in the position to determine when a conversation would be terminated and to terminate it without any warning. Ivanov was probably livid.

Amused by his former student's new-found self-confidence, Ivanov rang Skriabin. It was four in the morning in Moscow, but he knew the Russian was an early riser even when he consumed more than his share of vodka and cognac the evening before. Skriabin lived well. And why shouldn't he? He had joined the Communist Party and sold himself to the KGB. That meant a large apartment with all the latest technological gadgets, a big budget, and the right to travel to the West unaccompanied by KGB watchers and return with Western books. If Yevtushenko could get away with it, why couldn't he? As *quid* for the *quo*, he informed on his colleagues and on foreign visiting scholars. Ivanov knew that he had been the object of numerous reports written by Skriabin. Thanks to his Russian colleague's generosity—or, possibly, vanity—he had even read a handful and been impressed by their nuanced prevarications. Skriabin knew how to work the system. He was a heel, but a heel with a good heart, and a good scholar, which made all the difference.

"I scratch their backs," the sly Russian had once quipped, "and they mercifully refrain from scratching mine. No one gets hurt. They pretend to spy, I pretend to spy, but, in reality, it is all a game, a silly, stupid game invented by bored Party officials and underpaid KGB officers." And then adding, for good measure: "Besides, if I didn't, someone else would, and he'd be far less likely to be a good guy, a *muzhik*, than me."

Skriabin was delighted that his good friend had called. No, he laughed, he hadn't been to bed. As a matter of fact, he just got home—after an extended celebration in honor of some colleague's promotion. Ivanov knew the phone was bugged, but spoke openly anyway. His Russian friend was fascinated by the news—and deeply upset (Ivanov could imagine the crocodile tears streaming down his well-fed jowls). A colleague, a comrade, a friend—implicated in such a terrible scandal! But what could he do? he asked with intentional naiveté.

"Perhaps you could help him out of this mess?" Ivanov enquired, knowing that Skriabin would appreciate his indirection. "You have contacts, you have friends. One even hears that some of them might be influential."

"Consider the matter settled, my friend," Skriabin replied. It was time to go to bed. They chit-chatted for a few more minutes and then, before slipping under the covers next to his snoring wife, he called his contact at the secret police. It was terribly late, but, as the Chekists loved to say, the Soviet security services never slept.

*

Romanoff's predicament gave Ivanov no small satisfaction for another reason, one that he rarely discussed with his friends and colleagues. He usually fostered the impression that his official biography was accurate and that his family had left the Soviet Union after the Revolution. Technically, that wasn't a blatant untruth, but it would be more appropriate to say that they left some twenty-five years after the Revolution, in 1944 or 1945. Until then, they had lived in Estonia's capital city, Tallinn. Ivanov's parents had been school teachers in tsarist times and remained in the profession after Estonia became independent. Political turmoil and the Great Depression hit the country hard, but the Ivanovs managed, especially as they had relatives in the countryside who could be counted on to provide some vegetables and take care of the boy, Boris, during the summer months. Stalin's nonaggression pact with Hitler changed everything and, in 1940, Soviet troops marched into Estonia and claimed to liberate it from the fascists. The Baltic Germans, once a privileged minority in the Russian Empire, where they had occupied positions of authority in the armed forces, universities, and diplomatic corps and could retain their huge estates, had become a mere Soviet nationality, and a suspect one at that, in the 1940s. The Bolsheviks didn't trust them, so they made sure they were supervised by loyal Russians, Latvians, Poles, or Jews.

Hoping to keep a low profile, Boris's parents quit teaching—it had become too ideological and, thus, too dangerous—and became manual laborers in a local factory. Then came the Germans, whom everyone greeted with undiluted joy after the terrible vicissitudes of Stalin's brief revolution from above; then came the persecutions of the Jews, for whom few Baltic Germans-turned-*Volksdeutsche* felt great compassion; then came the Soviets again. The Ivanovs hadn't collaborated—though it wasn't clear just what the cousins in the countryside had done —but simply staying in occupied Estonia was enough to qualify one as a traitor—and, as both parents knew, traitors were summarily shot. Since the boy was with his relatives at the time the Soviets arrived, parents stayed in place, hoping against hope that all would be well.

It wasn't, of course. The executions of real and imagined collaborators began right away. As did the denunciations by pro-Soviet Estonians who had kept quiet all these years. As did, as well, the beatings and rapes of the Baltic Germans. Boris's mother was raped. So, too, were three of her cousins from outside Tallinn. When Boris's father asked if she could identify the culprit, she had simply answered, "Stalin." The front had advanced farther west, but the Ivanovs and their relatives resolved to get through and escape to Germany. The plan was only partially successful. Two relatives were shot by the Russians before they reached the front, one was executed by the SS as a deserter in Pomerania, and his father was captured by the Soviets near Berlin and deported to Siberia, where he presumably died. Miraculously, Boris and his mother survived and made their way to the United States in 1947, thanks to a distant relative in Germantown in eastern Pennsylvania who sent them an invitation and vouched to support them. Boris still remembered the first sight of the Statue of Liberty and the cawing of the seagulls as they approached Manhattan harbor.

That upstart Romanoff had always rubbed him the wrong way. Now Ivanov knew just why he had so instinctively disliked the boy genius. He was a rapist. He had raped German women. He could have raped my mother and my relatives, had he been there at that time. Perhaps he was, the sonofabitch, perhaps he was. In any case, it made no difference if he wasn't. His comrades were there—which meant that he, too, was there, in spirit if not in the flesh. He was a monster because they were monsters. Their actions were his, just as his were theirs. *"Do svidaniia,* Serge Romanoff," sneered Ivanov.

Ironically, Romanoff had never paid much attention to Ivanov or his ravings. The man was, in his view, little more than a frustrated academic who felt he had never gotten his due. Which was true, but only because he never deserved to get more than he got. Despite his sinecure at Yale, he was considered a hack by serious historians in Russia and Germany, the only two countries that, in Romanoff's estimation, consistently produced serious scholarship. Unfortunately, Ivanov had an obsession with him. Instead of working on his own research, he felt some bizarre need to attack Romanoff at every possible occasion. Initially provocative, his endless barbs soon made him into a predictable bore and laughing stock. Ivanov became his own worst enemy.

The only way to deal with such a lunatic was to ignore him, which Romanoff, much to Ivanov's frustration and anger, did. His American, Russian, or German colleagues would start with their Ivanov stories—the man was the butt of so many jokes that one entrepreneurial graduate student even compiled a collection and distributed it as a form of samizdat to his friends —and Romanoff, out of some combination of politesse, ennui, and indifference, would always raise his hand and say, "Stop, my friends. What's the use of laughing at children?" His admirable self-restraint pleased Romanoff. I am, he often thought, at the apex of my career. There is no reason for me to kick those hoping to climb to my heights. Let them fall of their own accord—as the vast majority invariably did.

*

Buckley passed on the information to his boss, who passed it on to his, until, finally, a decision was made somewhere in the middle levels of the Agency's Berlin office to assign one of its freelance informants, a West German journalist named Gisela Urban, to look into the matter. Find out if the charges are true, her contact had stupidly urged. Oh, really? she had wanted to answer. The Americans were arrogant and ignorant, the worst possible combination for people making big decisions, and the CIA's agents in Berlin were no different from the rest. Fresh out of some Ivy League school, usually Yale or Harvard, they spoke embarrassingly accented German, confused their conjugations and declensions, could never get the definite articles right, and, to top it all off, endlessly chewed bubble gum. How can anyone chew so much gum and blow so many bubbles? Didn't their jaws ever tire?

The Agency wanted to know whether the charges were damaging enough to enable them to trap Romanoff and force him to cooperate against the Reds. He traveled frequently to Russia and seemed to be on good terms with many influential Soviet officials. He could, if trained properly, prove to be a gold mine of intelligence—not about clandestine military affairs, but about personalities, trysts, gossip, the sort of stuff that all academics everywhere reveled in peddling. She was sure her CIA contact didn't see the deeper significance of the allegations. If they were verifiable and true—which, as she knew from her conversations with Bollow and the women, they probably were not —Romanoff's reputation would be tarnished beyond immediate repair and he'd lose his job at Harvard. Or, then again, considering how the stupid Americans dealt with moral complexities, he just might get a promotion.

Far more important were the implications for Germany. No one dared talk about the suffering of the Germans during the war. More than not daring to talk about this issue, no one knew *how* to talk about it without unleashing charges of anti-Semitism, pro-Nazi sentiment, nationalism, chauvinism, and so on. As a result, everyone in Germany and outside of Germany pretended that the assault on the Reich and its ultimate destruction had transpired without affecting the German population. It was, as the Americans liked to say, a harmless cakewalk. The problem with the allegations was that, even if unfounded, they forced people to stop pretending that nothing had happened. Some way of talking about German suffering would have to be found. Meanwhile, she'd have a wealth of information for a series of attention-grabbing articles.

That said, she'd have to keep as low a profile as possible —and that could get tricky. Urban's parents had escaped to West Germany from Leipzig in the late 1950s. Her father had been an engineer during the war and he appeared to have worked on rocket technology. The Communists had refrained from de-Nazifying him and, instead, had provided him with immediate employment in one of their research outfits, a tight-lipped institute on the eastern outskirts of Leipzig, situated near a huge underground bunker intended to safeguard the Party leadership in case of nuclear war. Her mother, a housewife with two children (Gisela's brother had been obliterated by Soviet tank fire at the Battle of Kursk), had been active in the *National Socialist-Frauenschaft* women's organization—perfunctorily, it seemed, but with sufficient visibility to make her susceptible to gentle persuasion by the East German secret police, the Stasi, which recruited her as a confidential informer.

Upon arriving in the West, Gisela's father was instantly hired by Siemens. Her mother found work as a kindergarten teacher. They had died in an automobile accident in 1972, while on the way to a vacation in Taormina. Some inebriated Italian in a mini-Fiat had struck them head on. Naturally, Urban couldn't be held accountable for the sins of her parents, but their ties to the Nazi establishment, their recruitment by the Stasi, and their possible continued service for the East German secret police after defecting to the West were sufficiently damnable to cast aspersion on Gisela's own ethical standards. The only thing worse than a Nazi or Communist collaborator was a Nazi *and* Communist collaborator.

Perhaps, she wondered, her research on behalf of the Agency should be a tad less exhaustive than her usual superlative product. Perhaps she should even drop the story as soon as possible, lest it blow up in her face. Why not let Bollow hang herself by herself? Sieglinde couldn't turn her back on a story she had broken. I never broke it, Gisela thought. I only reported on Romanoff's lecture. I was, thank God, just an innocent bystander who could, with a little luck and much caution, avoid getting embroiled in a scandal that could do me no possible good.

*

Skriabin's information had produced a similar effect on the Soviet side and, within a few hours of his conversation with his KGB contact, a thirty-five-year-old West German woman who had been drafted into the KGB's ranks of informers was assigned to the case. As an advanced graduate student specializing in Russian history at the Free University, Barbara Eichendorf could easily snoop around without drawing too much attention to herself —or to her work in the Revolutionary Red Army Faction.

The Soviet secret police sought her out after Baader, Ensslin, and Meinhof had been arrested and their other comrades, confused and fearful of imminent arrest, hid as deeply as they could in the underground. The KGB had little use for the RAF's —as well as the RRAF's—ideology. The young Germans suffered from what Lenin called "left-wing infantilism," believing that endless discussions were the way to make decisions and that a few bombs and leaflets could spark the revolution. No, serious Communists with a deep understanding of Marx and Lenin knew that a revolutionary upheaval required sustained agitational and organizational work with the masses conducted by a vanguard of dedicated professional revolutionaries who obeyed their leader unconditionally. Perhaps the Germans would grow up one day. Until they did, the Baader-Meinhof radicals were an anti-capitalist and anti-imperialist force that objectively served the interests of the Soviet Union, especially if supplied with money, arms, as well as refuge and training in the German Democratic Republic.

The KGB's attitude toward Eichendorf's group, the RRAF, was equally pragmatic. A blind man could see that they were children playing at revolution and that Eichendorf's endorsement of the German people's obliteration was too extreme, too reckless, and too unconsidered even for a security service that had no qualms about practicing genocide—but at home, with respect to its own subjects, and not abroad, where it could be misinterpreted as contradicting the Soviet commitment to peace. Since Eichendorf was a loose cannon, she would need close watching—and what better way to watch her than to employ her as both translator and informer?

The discussions in the Lubyanka did not end with Eichendorf's assignment to the case. Romanoff's file, forgotten after Mamontov's demise, was brought to light by one of the analysts tasked with providing some background on him. Consternation, confusion, and finger pointing followed, but, once tempers cooled and Colonel Lermontov, the veteran officer in charge of the matter, made it clear that no heads would roll— after all, the point was not to assign blame, but to aid the Fatherland—the file was perused and, much to everyone's surprise, they discovered that Romanoff had been the clandestine project of a certain Aleksei Mamontov for close to two decades.

On the one hand, that was good news. They had all the information they needed to understand just what made the man tick. Moreover, there'd be no need to recruit someone who already was, despite his inactive status, on the payroll. On the other hand, Romanoff's involvement with the KGB was dreadful news. If the imperialist press were to make the connection between him and Moscow, they'd have a field day blaming the Red Army and the Soviet leadership for the rapes in Berlin and elsewhere. Lermontov, a veteran KGB officer with distinguished service in Budapest in 1956 and Prague in 1968, knew how those hyenas operated. Once they had a tidbit promising to discredit socialism, they could be counted on to blow it out of all proportions, pursue avenues of investigation that, sooner or later, would uncover something genuinely embarrassing, and, before you knew it, they'd be accusing the USSR of violating human rights, committing war crimes, and so on—not just in Berlin, but in Budapest, where over half a million women had been raped, in Poland (that damned Katyń would inevitably be invoked), and —everybody's favorite—Prague, where the so-called spring of 1968, which portended winter for socialism, naturally had to be terminated.

Lermontov knew that the brouhaha would, like every storm, eventually pass and things would return to normal, especially where the pliant Germans were concerned. But this case could be different. It just might convince some otherwise friendly Germans to say something about the rapes. And then what? The German masses could be counted on to do nothing. They were too weak, too terrified, too subservient to their American masters. But fascist journalists and intellectuals would almost certainly exploit the violence to push their revanchist claims on western Poland, East Berlin, and the German Democratic Republic and question the Soviet Union's claim to have solved the "woman question."

Ironically, the key to the problem was a woman—more precisely, *this woman, eta zhenshchina*, this insufferable Sieglinde Bollow. It was her reporting that had created the mess in the first place. If she could be persuaded—gently, though decisively —that retracting the claims made by those five silly women was the proper thing to do—that it would promote peace, détente, and friendship between her country and the Soviet Union—then it was just possible that the damage could be undone and the scandal ended. Meanwhile, Romanoff could be reactivated and, with time, asked to provide some assistance to his country.

Eichendorf agreed to investigate Bollow, but not without reservations. Finding compromising material on her should be easy enough, as all of Springer's journalists were Nazis or had Nazi connections of some kind. What worried her was the KGB's motives. Were they trying to quash the story? Probably. It made sense, at least from their point of view. The revelations were an embarrassment to the Soviet Union, especially now that détente was in full bloom, the West Germans were courting Moscow, and the Baader-Meinhof comrades were subverting the Bonn regime's stability. The last thing the Kremlin wanted was a scandal of this kind and what the Kremlin wanted the KGB did. But that was no reason for the true vanguard of the revolution— the RRAF—to follow in the USSR's timid footsteps. Since history moved forward as a result of the contradictions engendered by the Marxian dialectic, this scandal, however inopportune for her Soviet employers and their bosses in Moscow, was precisely what she and her RRAF comrades needed. For them, it was a godsend, a once-in-a-lifetime opportunity to spit into the German public's face and to remind them that it was they, and not Hitler and his handful of henchmen, who exterminated millions in the war and the death camps.

She would have to tread carefully, providing the KGB with just enough accurate—as well as inaccurate or, better still, incomplete—information about Romanoff to create a sense of complacence, but without discrediting the allegations against him entirely. Perhaps the way to split the difference was to focus only on the two child victims—and thereby ignore or downplay Bollow as much as possible. The RRAF's case would be made if they were to admit guilt for the crimes their parents committed, while the KGB should be pleased with an outcome that would permit it to claim that Romanoff was a pedophile completely unlike the rest of his comrades in arms. Yes, she would have to tread very lightly and very carefully. Romanoff would be sacrificed on the altars of justice and socialism, but the professor was a small price to pay for historical inevitability to become a bit more inevitable a bit more quickly. Marx had claimed that Communists could "hasten the birth pangs of history." With a little luck, she and the RRAF would do just that.

CHAPTER SIX

Gisela Urban finally met all five women at a session of *Frauen für Frieden*. They had not expected, they confessed, their allegations to produce such a ruckus. They had come forward because the man in the *Berliner Zeitung* had raped them. They had had no political or other agenda. It wasn't even a question of justice or revenge, as none of them expected him to be arrested or the system to be shaken. It was simply a question of morality. Crimes had been committed. They had been the victims. And they had a moral responsibility to say that openly. As to the consequences of their revelations, they didn't matter. The important thing was to have acted in accordance with their consciences.

But that was also the problem. The two youngest victims had been children at the time of the assaults and were "almost positive" that Romanoff had been the assailant. The two oldest victims, the twins, were "absolutely certain" of his complicity, but both were old and, as everyone who knew them knew, they were often forgetful or misremembered. Only Maria Wurlitzer, who had been twenty at the time of the rape and was fifty today, could be considered reliable. But she had been political; she had opposed the regime; she had sat in prison. Her critics could easily assert she had a political axe to grind and was too subjective to be trustworthy.

There was also another problem. Despite their assertions of having simultaneously, and spontaneously, reacted to the photographs of Romanoff, it was actually Wurlitzer who had broached the issue of her rape—and theirs—*several months* before Romanoff even appeared on the scene. They had met and become friends at meetings of *Frauen für Frieden*. At one point, as the women were eating a *Kuchen* and sipping their coffees, as they always did at the end of their sessions, Wurlitzer had, for reasons she no longer remembered, broken her silence of thirty years and confided that she had been raped by a Russian in May of 1945, just after the war ended. The twins had chimed in, "We, too!" As did, a few minutes later, though more hesitantly, the two younger women, Ursula and Lotte.

Each then proceeded to describe her experience and, as they did so, Maria Wurlitzer had been struck by the refrain that their assailant had been a blond-haired, blue-eyed boy. Could it be that he was the same boy? As they tried to summon up their faded memories of those traumatic days, they progressively surmised that, yes, it was in all likelihood the very same boy. He was slim, they all remembered, and he was beautiful—not handsome, not good-looking, but beautiful. He smelled, but they all smelled, and he also had bad breath, but they all had bad breath. How many beautiful, blond-haired, and blue-eyed boys could there have been in the Russian army at that time? No, they concluded, it had to be one and the same assailant. The beautiful boy was, alas, a monster, a conclusion that saddened them until they realized—it may have been one of the twins who made the point —that most of the SS men were also beautiful, blond-haired, and blue-eyed. If our boys could be monsters, then so, too, could theirs. Didn't he have slanted eyes? the other twin enquired, but her interlocutors either ignored or didn't hear her and continued with their mutually reinforcing accounts.

The conversations would have remained on the level of intimate confessions had not Romanoff arrived in Berlin and been interviewed by the *Berliner Zeitung*. Wurlitzer was the first to have seen the photograph and to have determined to her satisfaction that this was the bastard. She then called Ursula, Lotte, and the twins and told them the news. They met an hour later in the restaurant at the elegant KaDeWe department store on Tauentzienstrasse and, just as they had made themselves comfortable and were about to eat—they had all ordered that day's special, a Wienerschnitzel with a potato and cucumber salad—

Maria fished out the newspaper from her canvas bag. "There he is!" she cried triumphantly. "That's him!" The twins had forgotten to bring their glasses, but, after borrowing Maria's, agreed that Romanoff was definitely the rapist. Both Ursula and Lotte mumbled something about the professor's not being quite as beautiful as they had remembered, but Maria assured them that, if they peered more closely at the photograph, they could easily see that, hiding behind the adult's visage, was the beautiful, blond-haired, blue-eyed beast that had attacked them amid the rubble of Berlin.

They agreed to contact Bollow as soon as they finished their lunch. The newspaper she worked for had some dubious connections with Axel Springer, but Bollow's articles—which all of them read despite their distaste for the paper that published them—were always objective and well-informed. Moreover, she had the solid appearance of someone who could be trusted. As one of the twins remarked, *"Diese Frau hat ein ehrliches Gesicht"*—"This woman has an honest face." Wurlitzer added that, although that was true, the best thing about Bollow was that she appeared to have retained her integrity while working for Springer. "She's tough," she noted, "and we need someone tough on our side." The others murmured their agreement.

In retrospect, as she told Urban, Wurlitzer suspected she may have influenced the women in their reception of the images. But she was absolutely certain that she had identified their assailant and, since it was understandable that the others might have faulty or incomplete memories, it was her sacred *duty* to facilitate their correct remembrance of those horrible days. Bollow agreed. The women's account had holes, but it was persuasive and, regardless of whether or not Romanoff was the culprit, the larger point, which had to be made no matter what, was that the Russians—and what was Romanoff if not a Russian?—had systematically engaged in mass rape. And that meant that all Russians were collectively guilty for the deeds of the actual assailants. After all, if all Germans were responsible for Hitler's crimes, then it followed that the same uncompromising logic and standards had to be applied to all other nations. Which meant that all Russian soldiers—indeed, all Russians—were rapists, just as all Americans had in fact dropped the atomic bombs on the Japanese.

After the story broke and the media turned their attention to the scandal, the twins felt frightened by the possibility of their becoming the targets of public scrutiny.

"We're old women," one of them pleaded, "so please keep us out of this."

"It's too late," Maria Wurlitzer reminded them. "We're all public figures now."

"Oh, dear, oh, dear," the other twin moaned. "I knew we should have stayed out of this."

"It's too late," Maria responded, quietly but firmly. "We all have to live with our choices, my dears. We chose to be silent for thirty years. Now, we finally chose to speak up. Besides, we have nothing to fear. We told the truth."

"Did we?" interjected one of the twins.

"We told the truth," Maria repeated, a bit more loudly and insistently. "It's the beautiful blond-haired, blue-eyed boy who should be terrified." The others said nothing. "Finally," Maria added, "finally, it's his turn. *Endlich ist er an der Reihe.*"

*

As she observed the group's dynamics, Urban sensed that a rift had formed between the four youngest and oldest women and Maria Wurlitzer. The former seemed nervous and uncertain and were unwilling to get involved in lengthy conversations. The latter had become even more assertive and self-confident than at the start. They were getting cold feet, Urban decided, which means that this story is headed for the ash heap unless some new twist emerges. That was good news for the professor and especially good news for her. She had made a splash, her editor was happy with her work, and sales had gone up. Her work was done and it was time to move on to other, less controversial and less dangerous, assignments.

Next day, Urban met her CIA contact at a Wurst stand at the Bahnhof Zoo station. Old enough to be her father, the bald man in the tightly bound trench coat hugged her perfunctorily and enquired loudly about her mother's health. She answered that all was well at home and then they strolled arm in arm to the nearby zoo. While he threw peanuts at the monkeys, she informed him of her findings—and doubts.

"There's definitely something to the story," she said, "and this Romanoff probably did something, but there's no real proof. It's four women with doubts and one woman without versus a respected Harvard professor. He'll deny everything. So would I, if I were in his place—even if I were guilty."

"Too bad," he offered. "You sure? Of course, you're sure. Too bad. Well, I guess you can't win them all." One of the monkeys smirked obscenely at them. "Anyway, the prof was a long shot. Keep your eyes peeled, OK? Maybe he'll take a wrong step and—"

"He's probably returning to the United States soon," she interjected. "There's little else I can do here, is there?"

"Oops," he clucked, feigning embarrassment, "forgot about that bit." He emptied the peanut bag and watched the pigeons swoop down. "Anyway, thanks. And stay in touch, OK?" Idiot, Urban thought, as he walked away. It was high time for the Agency to send him out to pasture.

She recalled promising Romanoff to review the women's testimony, but there was no need to divulge what she had learned from her conversations. Let him flail about and grow desperate, at least for a day or two. Unfortunately, the pleasure of imagining him squirm would be small consolation for the story's relegation to some dark corner of national memory. Over a million rapes wouldn't be ignored in other countries, but this was Germany and Germany, wracked by guilt, accused of every crime under the sun, torn between a far right and a far left, and reluctant to annoy either the Americans or the Russians, was special. The normal rules of political discourse didn't apply to a country that made the mass murder of Jews the centerpiece of its national identity. Other countries celebrated their achievements and ignored their stupidities and outrages. We were different. We were ashamed of our travails, we denied our achievements, and we trumpeted our crimes. It would take years, maybe decades, for Germany to become normal, like everyone else.

In the meantime, it was best for people like her to avoid rocking the boat and to live according to the unwritten rules of Germany's bizarre, and ultimately self-defeating, insistence on exceptionalism. The Nazis had also insisted on being exceptional. Her country would be best served by becoming as boring and as average as everyone else. But that would never happen as long as it, and its detractors, insisted it was uniquely different and had to pay the price for being so. Did they not see that, as long as we were exceptional, the Nazis would always be able to return—in our heads, if not in our streets?

Gisela had time and the animals were amusing, so she continued her stroll through the *Tiergarten*. If nations were animals, she mused, what would Germans be? Not monkeys: they were too unserious. We fancied ourselves as lions or tigers, but they won their battles while we lost ours. Rhinos were too single-minded. Giraffes were too complacent. We were, she decided, hippopotami: we had big jaws and huge asses and we threw our weight around, but in the end all we managed to do was to squash some poor creatures and produce a lot of muddied water.

As she strolled through the exotically constructed Elephant Gate, she thought she noticed a thin man in a rumpled striped linen suit following her. He had stood next to her near the hippos and smiled shyly when he caught her eye. An American? A Russian? A spy? He strode toward her and, hat in hand, gingerly enquired if she would do him the honor of having coffee with him at the Café Kranzler. Flustered and unnerved, she hesitated a second before responding sharply, too sharply: "*Nein, nein, nein!*" Shocked, he retreated like a kicked dog, mumbled his apologies, dropped his hat, fumbled with it as he picked it up, and then placed it backwards on his head. I am, she decided, becoming paranoid. This crazy city is making me incapable of distinguishing between an innocent come-on by some jerk and rehearsed performances by first-class manipulators.

*

Barbara Eichendorf had better luck. She ignored the twins and Wurlitzer and instead invited the youngest women, Ursula and Lotte, to lunch at the Paris Café on Kantstrasse. Favored by Berlin's intellectual set, the place might be sufficiently intimidating to make them more susceptible to her arguments. Normally, Eichendorf wouldn't be caught dead in such a bourgeois establishment, preferring the alternative scene in Kreuzberg or, when the mood struck her to go east, the working-class taverns near Käthe-Kollwitz Platz, but this, obviously, was an exceptional case that called for exceptional measures.

"Is this where you always lunch?" Ursula asked, struck by the shabbily elegant décor and its striking contrast to Eichendorf's student status.

"My professor has a large research budget," Barbara retorted without a moment's hesitation. "He's well connected"— she rolled her eyes to establish some distance between herself and him—"with the ministry." A sly grin followed. "I think we should comply with their wishes, don't you agree, ladies?" Like school girls, Ursula and Lotte nodded, obediently and enthusiastically.

The slim, mustachioed waiter took their order—escargots for Ursula, steak tartare for Lotte, and steak frites for Eichendorf, along with three glasses of an Alsatian red. While eating, they chatted about the weather, which was unusually warm for this time of year, the anti-war demonstrations in Frankfurt (the girls supported them), and American plans for arming Germany with nuclear weapons (they were opposed). The mood was friendly, they were at ease, and, rather than prolong the preliminaries that could erode their burgeoning trust, Eichendorf decided it was time to raise the issue on everyone's mind.

"Fashion?" Ursula quipped. Lotte giggled. The wine had not been without effect.

"No, the rapes." Barbara's eyes lost their sparkle and her voice became monotone. "I need to know. Pardon, my professor needs to know: did they really occur? Would you swear to their having occurred?"

"*Aber selbstverständlich!*" Ursula cried. "But, of course!"

"We *know* what we experienced, *Fräulein* Barbara," Lotte added, "and we experienced rape—a bloody, brutal, violent rape."

"Thank you," Barbara said, "that's what I—*we*—were hoping to hear." She opened her notebook and scribbled a few illegible words. "And now for the next question—excuse me, would you like another glass of wine? *Herr Ober!* Waiter!—yes, and now for the next question: Are you sure that the man who raped you is Professor Serge Romanoff?"

There was no answer, so she continued: "You said it was Romanoff who raped you when you were little girls. All you need to do is nod. That will serve as sufficient confirmation." She observed them expectantly, but both remained motionless.

Speaking slowly, Lotte broke the quiet. "He, well, looks like the boy I remember." Ursula nodded. "But how can we be absolutely sure?" Lotte asked. "You know we can't."

"And that's why we're so confused," Ursula interjected. "Our rights were violated, but is it fair to violate Professor Romanoff's? I don't know," she shook her head, "I just don't know."

"Neither do I," her sister added morosely.

This was going nowhere. The twins were fixated on themselves and had lost sight of the larger picture. Hoping to redirect their anger, Barbara reminded them of the mass rapes that had taken place, while emphasizing that they were only a minute part of the rape of Europe, the rape of Russia, the rape of Poland, the rape of Ukraine, and all the other innumerable rapes committed by Germans. "That made all Germans—including you and me—guilty and the guilt of the guilty can be expiated only by punishment. We deserved to suffer in Hell for all eternity, but God"—in whom Eichendorf did not believe for a second—"was merciful and, instead, rained down the bombs and bullets—and, yes, the rapes—as our punishment." The women appeared flustered and confused.

"Are you saying," Lotte asked hesitantly, "that we *deserved* to be raped?"

It wasn't yet time to answer that question. "Our punishment was appropriate to the crime," Eichendorf said. "We were all Nazis, after all, in some form or other—either willfully or not, either enthusiastically or not, either consciously or not." The women had turned a bright crimson and Barbara saw that her comment had struck a painful nerve. She would be direct, tighten the screws, and hope that her directness would shake loose the truth.

"You loved Hitler, didn't you?" The silence provided all the answers she sought. "You were both in the *Bund* and you both adored the Führer," she remarked matter-of-factly. Their embarrassment translated into an anxious fidgeting with their multiple rings and garish bracelets. They were defenseless, like sacrificial lambs, and it was time for the *coup de grâce*: "You are as responsible, as guilty, as Himmler, Rosenberg, and Goebbels. And yes, ladies"—Barbara waited a few tense seconds before completing her sentence—"*you deserved to be raped.*" One of them let out a barely audible cry before Barbara went for the kill. "As good Germans, as good Nazis, you *deserved* to be punished, because the only appropriate punishment for people who had wanted to rape Russia was to be raped by Russians."

A brief retreat—a calming of frayed nerves—was in order, so Barbara lied, because lies were permitted for the good of the cause. "I, too, was raped, but, to tell the truth, it set me free." She watched the women carefully and then added, "That punishment liberated me from the hell of modern Germany."

Lotte and Ursula appeared stunned, with puzzled expressions on their faces. Now there were six of them! Was there any woman in Berlin who hadn't been assaulted?

"Are you saying," Ursula's voice trembled slightly, "are you saying we should accuse the professor because—"

"—precisely because he stands for all the Russians who died in the war, whose deaths we all brought about, and who have a right—nay, an obligation!—to hate us and to punish us."

"By rape? Even by a rape he may not have committed?"

Eichendorf's patience was wearing thin. "He assuredly raped *some* German woman! It could just as well have been you! Don't you see? It's not about you as individuals or about him as an individual. It's about the collective guilt of every single German and the collective obligation of every single Russian to punish us." Her hands, pressed against the table, appeared to tremble. "Do you understand? *Verstehen Sie mich?* Forget yourselves! Forget Romanoff! It's about Germany, about Russia—ultimately, it's about humanity and our ability to start anew and build a better, more just society." Like her stepfather's during Sunday service, Barbara's voice rose in volume and pitch. "Look, the Russians *must* hate us and act on their hatred precisely because we *must* be hated in order to be saved. The bourgeois press and politicians condemn hate, but it's a healthy, purgative emotion. There must be hate as long as there is evil, because evil must be hated." And now her second *coup de grâce*: "*We Germans—all of us —must be hated because only hate will save us!*"

Speechless, Lotte and Ursula downed their wine and exchanged fearful glances. A bourgeois liberal would have stopped, moved by the prospect of impending tears, but a dedicated revolutionary had to push for final victory. Eichendorf continued her assault for another thirty minutes. Finally, two wet handkerchiefs and two more glasses of wine later, the women capitulated. They weren't quite sure they followed Barbara's logic, but the emotional force of her argument made sense. And she was right: it was time to make a clean break with the past, not by denying it, but by accepting absolution and doing penance. They would sign a statement stating that Romanoff, "acting on behalf of the entire Russian nation had fulfilled his moral duty" by raping them, but insisted that it not be revealed to the public

—or not yet. They were tired and fearful of publicity, even as both admitted that, contrary to their expectations, they did feel lighter, less burdened, by their exchange. Perhaps Barbara was right about the liberation that flowed from contrition?

As Barbara Eichendorf rode the tram to her flat off Clayallee, in Berlin's southwest, she resolved that the signed statement should be mysteriously leaked—to the Springer press, of course—as soon as possible. Her KGB handlers would be angry, but her group's goals would be advanced. If the women confronted her, she'd blame the absent-minded professor. Besides, when faced with the revelation, the KGB would have to disavow Romanoff as a pervert, which, in the final analysis, would be to his benefit as well. The Americans, who all led perverted lives under their Wild West capitalism, would never notice. They might even elect him President.

*

Bollow and Romanoff met, on his prompting, in the same restaurant in Kreuzberg, where their acquaintance had begun. That was Romanoff's idea and, as she correctly surmised, it was his way of proposing they start over again. Predictably, he was sitting at the same table in the back corner, with the same oversized plant shielding them from the curious eyes of the other guests. A large Turkish family, the stocky women dressed in traditional attire, the wiry men wearing starched white shirts and unpressed black suits, was celebrating something at the other end and provided a steady drumroll of conversation that enhanced their seclusion.

His goal was to persuade her by indirection that he was *schwul*. Hers was to determine the origins of the scar above his right eye. He decided to wear a pair of tight-fitting jeans, white socks, penny loafers, and a flowery silk shirt, which he had bought at the KaDeWe. He considered a speckled red-orange bandana, but decided that would be too obvious and lead her to think something was afoot. She came in her usual attire— jeans, cotton shirt, and tasseled leather bag. Romanoff laughed inwardly as he considered that they could actually have passed for a couple. It was too late to adopt a swish or certain limp-wrist mannerisms; he'd have to be as direct as his commitment to indirection made possible and hope for the best. Fortunately, he could probably count on her wanting to believe that his indifference to her seductive efforts was a symptom of his sexual proclivities.

His efforts met with failure almost immediately. Sieglinde was in no mood for subtleties and she paid no attention whatsoever to his dress. Instead, she seemed determine to have a serious conversation, which was the very last thing he wanted. A gay Berliner had to be, well, gay, in the traditional sense of the word. Sieglinde's seriousness was not what he had expected. In turn, she was annoyed by his overly obvious attempt to be flippant and superficial. And what was his absurd attire all about? Didn't he realize he had all the earmarks of a flaming gay man? Where did he think we were—on Nollendorfplatz?

Romanoff fell into a deep funk after seeing that his efforts had patently failed. Their rendezvous had become pointless and, were it not for his old-school upbringing, he would have been inclined to act as any hot-blooded American male would and leave. Not storm out. That would be gauche. But just rise from his seat, throw a few marks onto the table, say "*Auf Wiedersehen*," and make a crisp about-face and head for the exit. That way, he'd preserve some of his dignity intact. But he remained riveted to his chair, holding the menu in both hands, staring at the illegible text, and wondering what to do next.

Bollow felt equally awkward. They were supposed to have embarked on a serious conversation, both to clear up the mystery of the scar and to prepare themselves for the interview, which she hadn't forgotten, even though he apparently had. Instead, Harvard's star professor sat before her like a small boy who'd been caught taking cookies from the cookie jar. He squirmed in his seat, kept his mouth shut, and stared fatuously at the menu, which he actually managed to hold upside down. Their embarrassment had become palpable and Sieglinde considered excusing herself, going to the ladies' room, and exiting by the back door. But she couldn't. The interview could wait; indeed, it could be forgotten. The scar could not. It was best to take the proverbial bull by its horns.

"That scar above your right eye," she stated. "How did you get it?"

That was the signal for a thaw. Romanoff instinctively raised his hand to the scar and rubbed it. "In the war, I think," he mumbled. "I'm not sure when. Maybe after the war. I worked as a laborer in Germany after I defected. It could have been some accident." He rubbed the scar again. "Or was it the war? I honestly don't remember."

"One of the women says she kicked you while you were trying to climb on top of her. She says she caused the scar and she says she remembers the blood on your face."

He had regained much of his composure and unhesitatingly declared, "*Quatsch*."

"Is it really nonsense? She swears to it. And if she's right, then the scar puts you at the scene of the crime. Then it's no longer just her word against yours." Sieglinde leaned forward. "You understand the seriousness of the charge, don't you?"

"Of course, I do. Even so," he maintained, "it's *Quatsch*," and removed a cigarette from his case.

"You really don't remember where you got the scar?" Her tone was becoming plaintive and that irritated her. After all, she was the prosecutor and he was the defendant. "Help me—please. I think you're innocent, but this makes you look bad—very bad."

He appeared to be, or possibly was, thinking. "It must have been the war. We crawled through barbed wire, fought our way through dense forests and bushes. Everyone had cuts and scratches." His eyes swept the room and momentarily settled on the shrieking Turkish children playing tag. "Should we order? Maybe just drinks?" His gaze returned to her again. "It surely was no kick to the forehead. For one thing, I didn't rape those women. You'll just have to accept that—or not. For another, how could she have kicked an assailant in the forehead? In the shins, yes. In the, er"—and he pointed to his crotch—"also yes. But the forehead? She'd have to be over two meters tall and the assailant would have to be tiny. And I'm not exactly short and my guess is that she's not exactly tall. So, you see, '*quod erat demonstrandum*'."

Sieglinde leaned back, lit a cigarette, and considered his argument. It was not unpersuasive. The twins were of below average height for German women, about five feet three inches by American standards, and the professor was just under six feet. He might have been shorter then, but, even so, the case for the scar's being the product of a well-placed kick seemed thin, in fact, much thinner than it had initially seemed. At the same time, there was no denying that all soldiers had scars from the fighting. Why should Romanoff be any different? Why should his explanation not be considered to be true barring convincing evidence of its being false?

Her deliberations were interrupted by the rotund Turk who took their order and bowed with exaggerated decorum. Their rakis arrived quickly and they raised their glasses and drank, as Sieglinde indelicately proposed, to truth. Romanoff lips assumed a sardonic twist, but he tapped his glass gently against hers. The tension had disappeared. They were on speaking terms again and his embarrassment had vanished. They downed their drinks—she, evidently, had needed one as well—and Romanoff ordered two more.

He leaned back and decided to be as frank as she had been. "I want to apologize," he said, figuring that such an opening line would be an effective way of disarming her and getting the advantage. "For the other night."

She was conspicuously embarrassed and Romanoff could have sworn she turned the color of the Soviet flag. "Forget it," she mumbled. "Just forget it. It's not important."

"It *is* important," he insisted, the two fingers with the cigarette raised like exclamation points. "I find you very attractive, but…" His voice trailed off and his fingers returned to the table. He was beginning to feel uncertain about how to continue. He didn't want to say he was *schwul*; he only wanted her to come away with the impression. But how does one create that impression in a Turkish restaurant in Kreuzberg? She had plainly not been impressed by his costume. Perhaps they should have met in a bar off Nollendorfplatz? But that would have been too obvious, too direct, too forced. I don't know how to proceed, he concluded sadly. I have no idea whatsoever. I am lost.

"I understand," she said, discomfited by his statement and hoping to move on to some other topic. Why did Romanoff persist in raising this issue from the dead? Did he really think that a woman like her, one who had lived in the Berlin of the 1960s, hadn't had her share of failures as well as successes? Did he really think she was hurt or depressed or upset by his rejection? And then her eye caught his shirt and she had the epiphany he had been hoping for, but with a twist that he had not expected. *He wants me to think he's gay!* Bollow almost laughed out loud. He actually thinks that the only way he can save face is by pretending to be uninterested in women! A world-famous Harvard professor—and he could think of nothing better! The man was, she decided, a child, no, a teenager, a blond-haired, blue-eyed teenager. Or was he playing a double game? Was he trying to plead innocence over the rapes by pretending to be a homosexual? But, if that were the case, did that not mean that he knew he had something to hide? Was he guilty, after all? Whatever the case, the professor was a liar and couldn't be trusted.

Sieglinde resisted the impulse to leave, rush home, and write another article, one exposing his underhanded dealings. She knew she couldn't write such a piece. There was no evidence —only hearsay and supposition on her part. She'd also have to reveal too much about her own life and her relationship with Romanoff to make any of the suppositions sound plausible and she wasn't willing to do that. In the end, he had made a good case defending himself against the charges, the women's testimony wasn't quite as airtight as it had originally seemed, and his playacting at being homosexual would be dismissed as the idiosyncratic behavior of a professor who'd spent too much time in musty archives.

She barely heard Romanoff's chattering. Nervous and feeling insecure, he rushed through a slew of topics ranging from Berlin's architecture (dreadful) to Baader and Meinhof (horrifying) to Brezhnev (sad) to Watergate (tragic) to the origins of Russia in the cradle of civilization he called Rasha. He spoke elegantly, persuasively, and almost automatically. Her extended silence worried him. She was obviously playing through some scenarios in her mind and wasn't listening. But neither was he. After some thirty more minutes of persiflage, he stopped and asked, "Should we get the check?" She nodded and, upon exiting, they parted, each going in a different direction, thankful that the ordeal was finally over.

The story was dead, Sieglinde resolved as she descended the stairs to the U-Bahn. The tiles were covered with meaningless squiggles and outdated posters and the station smelled of stale urine. Two alcoholics sat in a corner, swinging beer bottles to the tune of their off-key rendition of Beethoven's Ode to Joy. The melody lingered in her memory, as she took a seat and the doors closed. As did her eyes. She had done her paper a great service by bringing to life an issue—the suffering of Germans in the war—that no one in the political establishment, and especially those on the left, felt comfortable talking about. Her editor would be happy and she might expect some juicier assignments in the future. But pursuing the professor was a dead end, even though he was evasive, albeit persuasive and logical, and probably had something to hide.

But who didn't? Which German or Russian who experienced and survived the war did not do or see or hear things that would make one's blood curdle? We had all suffered and we were all guilty, some more than others, but we were all guilty of committing some action that in peacetime would be considered a heinous crime. The Russians in particular bore a heavy burden of guilt. They had supported Lenin and his atrocities; they had supported Stalin and his barbarities; and then they had behaved toward the Germans—even if understandably—just as the

Germans had behaved toward them. The Russians had bathed themselves and their neighbors in blood for much of the twentieth century. And what of earlier centuries? Russia had been a synonym for genocide since at least Ivan the Terrible. How many Siberians, Georgians, Armenians, Ukrainians, Poles, and Central Asians had died in Russia's expansionist wars? We were worse than them during the last war, but their record over the last five hundred years was infinitely worse than ours. That was no consolation, however, and, self-evidently, no excuse for Hitler.

She opened her eyes. Sitting opposite her in the subway was a pretty boy—his blond locks curled above his forehead, his azure eyes staring dully at some spot to her left. Could such an Adonis be capable of rape, especially when he could have any girl—or boy—he wanted? He returned her smile, though far less confidently, and, reddening, promptly turned his gaze away. But this was peacetime, whereas the rapes had taken place during war. Men acted differently during war, as did, presumably, women. Equipped with a uniform, rifle, bayonet, and grenades, they were ordered to violate civilization's edicts and enjoy killing. If they refused to kill, they would be shot. Only saints had the moral fortitude to say no and accept the consequences. Normal human beings hung low their heads, marched off to the front, and tried to annihilate the enemy before the enemy, having received the identical equipment and orders, attempted to annihilate you. Why should someone who'd been killing for years believe that rape was more impermissible than slitting throats, disemboweling men, or dousing them with flamethrowers? The boy winked at her as he exited. If I were younger, she resolved, I'd follow him—but now I am too old, too tired, and too knowledgeable.

*

Depressed and demoralized, Romanoff watched Berlin's buildings, signs, and traffic lights merge into a blur and flash by as his taxi sped toward the Kempinski. The meeting with Bollow had been an unmitigated disaster. She had seen through his game.

He had stuttered through the encounter, talked nonsense for most of the time, and failed to achieve anything. As a matter of fact, he probably achieved the very opposite of what he had intended and, in all likelihood, she came away persuaded that his incompetent performance was merely a cover-up for his complicity in the rapes. What would happen next? Probably a flurry of additional articles, additional accusations, and additional embarrassment. Harvard and his department must have learned of the scandal by now. Tongues were surely wagging there, as well as in all the history departments of North America and Western Europe, and that reprehensible worm Ivanov was surely basking in his competitor's sullied glory. Was his career ruined? No, not yet, but it was moving rapidly in that direction. A few more twists in the story and he would be finished as a scholar.

So many years, so much effort—all for naught. His German colleagues had promised to help, but, being fair-weather friends, they had to be calculating the costs and benefits of too close an association with a drowning man and concluding that distance was advisable. The journalist Urban had also offered her help, but she, too, had doubtless decided to keep her distance. I am—Romanoff's conclusion struck him as all too obviously true—a pariah, a leper. Soon, maybe very soon, I'll be completely isolated and, then, even if I am vindicated, it will be too late.

And what an irony! They will be hanging me for crimes I almost definitely did not commit, while continuing to ignore those that I definitely did commit. But why the qualifier, almost? The case against the twins' claim to have kicked him was conclusive. The case for his having received the scar in the course of the war was extremely plausible, almost air tight. And yet it didn't matter. The five women were more likely to be believed than he was. They were sympathetic, they were frail, they had suffered. As for me, I merely fought in one of the bloodiest wars in world history. I saw and did things that no one should see or do. But, just as the war excused my deeds, so, too, it made them less worthy of commiseration than the suffering of civilians. Soldiers were damned. Whatever they did, they were damned. They were damned simply by being soldiers who were taught to kill.

Very well, the situation was hopeless or nearly so. What, then, should he do? Return to Harvard in shame? Tolerate the snickers of colleagues and students? Get fired? Stay in Germany and endure the same abuse? Defect to the USSR? Now *that*, he snorted, would be poetic justice—to return to the country he had abandoned or, more accurately, had been ordered to abandon. The Soviets might be uneasy about the allegations, but would probably dismiss them as imperialist propaganda intended to blacken a first-class Russian *muzhik*. He'd probably get a job at some university. Not in Moscow or Leningrad, however: there'd be too many Western journalists poking around for a salacious story. They'd send him to Tashkent or Vladivostok, at least until the scandal blew over. Or they might just decide to leave him there forever. He shuddered at the thought. On the other hand, Uzbek rice and lamb *plov* was tasty, Vladivostok had excellent fish, and anything might be preferable to the opprobrium awaiting him in the United States or Europe. Were these his only choices? Good God, apparently so. Perhaps he should consider suicide? No, that would be admitting guilt and, besides, he was too much of a coward to do something quite that extreme.

As the car passed the KaDeWe and neared the ruins of the Kaiser Wilhelm Memorial Church, his ruminations were unceremoniously interrupted by a loud boom followed by screams and a column of smoke. Sirens instantly filled the air and police cars flooded the streets. The driver advised him to get out and go the rest of the way on foot.

"Traffic will be a mess," he declared gloomily. "I may be stuck here for an hour."

"*Eine Bombe?*" Romanoff asked.

"Probably," he shrugged. "It's probably those crazy terrorists." He lifted his shoulders and tilted his head. "This country is *verrückt*—crazy. They think they're revolutionaries, but they're just crazy. And what are people like me supposed to do? I have a wife, I have kids, I have—" Romanoff slipped out, shut the door, and hurried away.

The bomb appeared to have gone off in front of the Beate Uhse sex shop near the Bahnhof Zoo station. Several ambulances had gathered inside the police cordon and the sirens continued blaring. Why would left-wingers try to destroy a store that specialized in sex toys? Wasn't free love part of their agenda? Didn't untrammeled sex subvert bourgeois morality? Romanoff decided against viewing the site more closely and veered left toward the Ku'damm. When he arrived at the Kempinski, he headed straight for the bar and, after greeting the female bartender, ordered a double Bombay martini. With olives? she asked. No, definitely not, he answered. He needed undiluted, unadulterated alcohol. Perhaps, if he were completely inebriated, he'd be able to figure out how to get out of this mess.

CHAPTER SEVEN

One of the immediate consequences of the bomb blast was the *Polizei*'s decision to arrest prominent leftists with a declared sympathy for the Red Army Faction. The *Bullen* raided apartments, cafés, and bars known to be radical hang-outs and took some fifty, mostly ungroomed women and men into custody. The women were in the majority, as they were within the Baader-Meinhof group and among its sympathizers —a sign, as some elderly Germans liked to say, of the growing equality between the sexes: now women, too, had become murderers.

Amid the first radicals to be caught in the dragnet was Barbara Eichendorf, who, true to character, put up quite a fight before being subdued by three bulls. Her arrest would not have merited particular attention had it not been for one detail: she was carrying the signed affidavits of the two rape victims she had interviewed. The policeman who searched her wasn't sure what to make of the document, but it had the appearance of something official and, hence, important; moreover, it looked cryptic and, in these dangerous times, he had to assume the worst and pass it on to the counter-terrorism unit in the Ministry. For all he knew, it could be nothing more than a bombastic manifesto; but it could also be a set of coded instructions for an act of terror. The official whose desk served as the document's temporary resting place glanced at it, realized it had something to do with that Russian historian who was embroiled in an ongoing scandal, and concluded it was above his pay grade and should be passed on to the German security service, the *Bundesnachrichtendienst*, which maintained a low-profile presence in West Berlin.

Siegfried Leitner, the sallow-skinned, chain-smoking BND official who perused the document was, like many of his colleagues, an agent of influence of the KGB—a status conferred on individuals who could be relied on to have the interests of the Soviet Union at heart—and he quickly realized that the document could serve the interests of both the USSR and West Germany. This Eichendorf *Weib* was a pain in West Germany's ass. The BND knew of her extremist ideological views and it kept track, as best it could, of the little-known RRAF, but had thus far found no evidence to incriminate her. By the same token, if made public, this document would only add to the Kremlin's already acute embarrassment at having participated in a wave of atrocities after the war. If the KGB could provide some dirt on Eichendorf, thereby enabling the German authorities to dispose of her in Stammheim, then the West German authorities might be more than happy to return the favor and make the document disappear.

The *quid pro quo* was obvious, as well as in everyone's obvious interest. All Herr Leitner had to do was to convince both sides to agree to this simple exchange. That was accomplished easily enough. The anonymous official in the Ministry's counter-terrorism unit gave his approval immediately, on the grounds that anything Eichendorf touched had to be suspicious. Colonel Lermontov in Moscow also had no objections to seeing the bothersome matter be put to rest. Romanoff's *bardak* was effectively over, even though he didn't know it.

Surprisingly, the normally imperious Eichendorf lost her cool and protested loudly and vehemently. She knew her rights, she shouted, her face flush with anger, and the fascists had no right to take her belongings. She even recited the first article of Germany's Basic Law—that "human dignity shall be inviolable." The guards ignored her and her rants, her inmates were annoyed by a revolutionary's bizarre invocation of a capitalist tract, and, very soon, her protests ceased and she sat glumly on a bench with several other comrades.

"Man kann mit den Faschisten nicht sprechen," one of them

pointed out matter-of-factly. "One can't speak with the fascists." Then he chided her: "You should know that."

"*Besser ruhig bleiben*," another advised. "Better to be quiet. They can't hold us for long without charges. And they have nothing to charge us with."

"Does anyone know who set the bomb?" Eichendorf asked, hoping to change the subject. "Our people would never attack a sex shop. Was it a police provocation?"

The inmates laughed and nodded. "What else? You know how the *Bullen* operate."

"Pathetic," Barbara shook her head in seeming disbelief.

"But still very dangerous." All heads went up and down in agreement.

*

Romanoff left the hotel bar several hours later, completely blotto, and staggered toward the Bahnhof Zoo station, where he hoped to have a curry Wurst and beer. The police cordon was still in place, but the crowds were gone, the sex toys had been removed, and the window was being replaced by two workmen in orange overalls. Despite the copious amounts of alcohol—martinis, cognac, and whiskey—he had imbibed, he was, unsurprisingly, no nearer a solution to his problems. It was hopeless, but he was hungry and hung-over and it was better to be sated and feel despair than to be hungry and feel despair.

He devoured the sausage and, as he cradled the beer bottle and surveyed the other denizens of the ill-lit station, one of them, a heavy-set man with a handlebar mustache and long red hair, glared at Romanoff and shouted, "*Was willste?*" Romanoff wanted nothing—he may not even have heard the question or realized it was directed at him—so he said nothing and grinned in the stupid manner of someone who has not yet fully recovered from several hours of excessive alcohol consumption. The man climbed to his shaky feet, grabbed an empty brown beer bottle, and, walking unsteadily, approached Romanoff, who, still oblivious of what was transpiring before his eyes, continued to grin and sip his beer. The grin appears to have enraged the man, who stumbled toward the unsuspecting professor and swung the bottle against the side of his head. Romanoff didn't even have time to produce a moan before he crumpled to the ground like a sack of potatoes. The assailant, along with everyone else in the hall, took to flight, while the turbaned man who ran the Wurst stand, a recently arrived Sikh with an elementary knowledge of German and no papers, ran up the stairs and boarded the first S-Bahn. Someone eventually called for an ambulance and Romanoff was rushed to the Charité hospital. Several stitches and a few aspirins later, he was asleep in a room with five other patients.

They released him next day. Gisela Urban was waiting in the lobby, in her capacity as semi-friend and journalist. She asked him what happened and, as the haggard and unusually rumpled Romanoff began preparing an answer in his aching head, it dawned on him that the unfortunate assault by some drunken hooligan just might serve to save the day.

"He came at me with a bottle and threatened to kill me," he said dryly.

"Who was he? Do you know? Did he say why he wanted to kill you?"

"I never saw the man before," Romanoff replied. "But he said he was paying me back, that this was revenge." Would she buy the line?

"Pay you back for what?" Urban enquired. "Revenge for what?"

"For violating German womanhood."

"Those were his exact words?"

"Those were his exact words." He adopted a slight frown and pretended to be immersed in painful introspection. "I think I'll sue the newspaper for having incited some crazy Nazi to assault me."

"How do you know he was a Nazi?"

"Who else," he answered, "would speak of German womanhood?" And then the punchline, seemingly delivered as an afterthought: "He shouted 'Heil Hitler' as he rushed me. Needless to say, I was terrified, absolutely terrified." Then he added for dramatic effect: "He could have killed me." Would she accept his version of what transpired?

She did. "This changes everything," she said, certain that her story would trump anything Bollow could come up with. "Would you do me a favor and tell no one about this? I'd like it to be an exclusive of the *Berliner Zeitung*."

Romanoff twisted his lips and produced what he hoped was a gracious, and not vain, smile. "Of course. And if you need any more quotes, you know where to reach me."

Excited by her coup, Urban rushed off, while Romanoff bought an espresso in the coffee machine, took a seat in the antiseptic waiting room, and feigned absorption in last month's copy of *Der Spiegel*. This could just be his lucky day. If the article appeared in today's afternoon edition, he'd be converted from villain to victim and Bollow and her co-conspirators would be exposed as vicious harridans out to destroy an innocent historian.

That would be too bad: Sieglinde was a fine woman, as decent and honest as a journalist could be. But she was also a manipulative liar who had trouble distinguishing between genuine sincerity and playacting. He had tried to be forthcoming with her, but her maddening silence, her searching eyes, and her noncommittal remarks had proven to be too much for him to bear. People like her couldn't be trusted to refrain from destroying lives for the sake of career advancement. He had tried reason; he had appealed to emotion. Nothing had worked. Now it was time to play, as the Americans so nicely put it, hard ball. He returned the magazine to the coffee table and surveyed the room. The people occupying the other seats all had long faces or teary eyes. He wanted to laugh, to give full expression to the elation he was feeling, but, out of deference for their suffering and sensibilities, refrained from doing so.

When the police arrived, he told them exactly what he had told Urban. They would, they implied, characterize the assault as a hate crime attributable to Germany's stubbornly vigorous neo-Nazi underground. He signed some document and they left, expressing their hope that the incident would not jaundice his attitude toward their city. It would not, he assured them. Several hours later, his headache gone and his mood decidedly brighter, Romanoff strolled into the lobby of his hotel and encountered a gaggle of journalists with pens, pads, and cameras. There was even a television crew. Urban was smiling broadly and, as he ostentatiously kissed her on both cheeks and embraced her, she showed him the paper. *"ATTENTAT AUF PROFESSOR!"* screamed the red-and-black, upper-case headline. *"Herr Professor! Herr Professor!"* cried the journalists. Like an actor in full command of his craft, Romanoff stepped into their midst and, speaking in high-brow German, explained just how he had narrowly escaped a violent death at the hands of some fascist fanatic.

"I fear," he said in summary, "that he was inspired to perform his brutal act by the slanderous stories about my activity here in Berlin in May 1945. Let me be perfectly clear"—it occurred to Romanoff that he had just purloined one of Richard Nixon's favorite lines—"let me be perfectly clear: I never committed the heinous crimes that the five women in question have unjustifiably, and inexplicably, accused me of committing. I do not doubt for a second that they were brutally assaulted. I do not doubt for a second that crimes were committed. But I am not the perpetrator." He sensed he had the journalists in his hands. The questions that followed were polite and restrained. So far, Romanoff concluded, so good.

*

Romanoff's performance with the press left Gisela Urban feeling depressed and distraught. Arrogant, self-serving, and emotionless, he had prattled on and on about himself and his work, at one point embarking on a mind-numbing discussion of his path-breaking work on the origins of something called Rasha and creating the impression that he was utterly indifferent to the five women whose lives had been so deeply affected by the assaults they experienced thirty years ago. Didn't he realize that this impromptu press conference wasn't about him and his putative innocence—after all, she had established that in the article—but about them, the women? *Feingefühl*, a feeling for nuance and delicacy, was all it took and Romanoff had conclusively demonstrated that he lacked it altogether. Small wonder that her colleagues in the press corps had grown silent and, after Romanoff had finished his peroration, had nothing to say. They were stunned by his insensitivity and boorishness, just as she was. The man might be innocent and he may have been the target of an assassination attempt and he may be a deservedly celebrated scholar, but he was also a brute—despite the appearance of gentility that he cultivated.

Some of her colleagues approached her for inside information, but she had none—which was true—and they made a hasty exit to search for other sources. As the crowd in the lobby thinned, Urban's eye fell on a thin young man with upturned nose and metal-rimmed glasses who was wearing khaki slacks, maroon penny loafers, a striped college tie, a button-down white shirt, and a navy-blue jacket with a gold insignia. It was John Buckley, an agent of the CIA whom she had met at several book readings and musical performances at Amerika Haus, the U.S. information center housed in a dull modernist building near the Bahnhof Zoo. He was sitting on a leather couch and observing the few remaining journalists milling about aimlessly. He casually waved at her and revealed his gleaming teeth.

"That was, uh, quite a show," he observed. "Not sure what to make of it. Any ideas?" His insistence on speaking in incomplete sentences had always annoyed her, so she decided to respond in kind.

"No idea."

His face exuded disappointment and confusion; perhaps for that reason, complete sentences returned. "I mean, was he *trying* to look bad?"

"What else would you expect from a Harvard professor

who's received accolades on both sides of the Atlantic?"

"Yeah, I suppose so."

"But surely you're not here to discuss our friend's relationship with the German media."

A hesitant smile briefly graced his face. "No, of course not. It's something else." He lowered his voice and bent his head toward her. "We've learned from one of our sources—"

"Who?" she demanded. "A journalist?"

"Can't say, top secret. Well, not really—a guy in the BND." He laughed quietly. "It's funny, really. He informs on the Russians for us and on us for the Russians. He's got the system beat. A win-win, whatever happens, right?"

"Right."

"You know," he said distractedly, "you Germans get me. You're willing to work for the angels and for the devils. Sooner or later, you'll have to take sides, you know. It's either us or them, right?"

"Right." Alas, the insufferable Buckley really was right. "It's our history, our political culture." She stopped her apologia. "Sorry, I interrupted you...."

"Right, yes—as I was saying, one of our sources, this two-faced fellow in your spy service, told us that his people and the Russians have been talking about some kind of deal involving Romanoff. Would you like a coffee or something?" She shook her head. "The russkies are getting worried about the bad press their heroic soldiers are getting. Whatever Romanoff did or didn't do, there's suddenly all this talk of Russians going berserk and raping millions of German *Frau*'s. Looks bad, especially for a peace-loving country like the Soviet Union that wants to suck the West dry."

"So, they want the scandal to go away," she concluded.

"Bingo!"

"And the Germans want the same thing, because they're uncomfortable talking about German victims in the war."

"Bingo again!"

"So, how can they put the toothpaste back into the bottle?"

"You mean tube," he corrected her. "Ah, this is where it gets a tiny bit complicated. One Barbara Eichendorf—"

"The radical lefty?"

"That's the one! Well, this Eichendorf lady got herself arrested after the bombing of the sex shop." Buckley snorted. "God, only a German terrorist would throw a bomb at a sex shop. Anyway, she got herself arrested while carrying on her exalted person a document—"

"A document?" she demanded. "What kind of document?"

"If you'd stop interrupting me, I'll tell you," he said impatiently. "It's a signed affidavit," he continued, "—the two youngest women signed it—saying they're sure he done it. Mucho embarrassing for the prof, of course, but also no great shakes for our russki and kraut friends. Makes everyone look bad—and I mean really, really bad." He scratched his head. "So, what is to be done?" His eyes brightened. "Hey, wasn't that something Lenin wrote?" Urban nodded. "See? College paid off, right? Well, anyway, this is where the grand bargain comes in. Everyone needs to get Eichendorf out of the picture, preferably into some deep dungeon." He rubbed his hands. "Gosh, this is good. Wish I had thought of it. So, the russkies have agreed to provide your people with evidence of Eichendorf's being an informer for the KGB and —"

"Is that for real? Is she really a KGB spy? I can't believe it."

"Believe it, my children, and ye shall be saved." His silly grin morphed into a glassy expression. "For years, apparently."

"So, her radicalism was all for show?"

"*Nyet*," he replied, "that seems to be for real—it's crazy, yeah, but for real."

"So," Urban summed up, "Eichendorf goes to jail, the document is destroyed, the professor is saved, and all of us can go back to pretending that the Russians were angelic liberators who were welcomed with flowers and champagne by the smiling womenfolk of Berlin in May of 1945."

"Neat, right?"

"Yes, neat. And what's in it for you?"

"Harvard's name remains spotless and American scholarship rides into the sunset."

"Is that all?" she asked slyly. It wasn't all and she knew what he would say in response.

"And the good professor, overwhelmed with gratitude to the Agency, volunteers his services to us in the Cold War. As I said, neat—right?"

"And the women? Off to the ash heap of history with them?" Urban purposely used the Soviet metaphor.

"Good Lord, no!" he cried. "They shall be feted for their bravery—in the good ol' U.S. of A. We were thinking of a speaking tour, maybe a few awards, citations, perhaps an honorary doctorate from some small liberal arts college in the middle of nowhere. The Poles, the Ukrainians, oh, and especially the Germans will love them. Ours, naturally, not yours."

"Everybody wins," she said without enthusiasm.

"Everybody wins *hands down*," Buckley beamed. "And," he added in confidence, "I probably get a promotion. Come to think of it, you will, too. We'll see to it." He rose from the couch, straightened his tie, and grinned, "Don't look so glum. We all win."

"Except for the truth," she observed caustically.

"Oh, that!" he giggled. "Let the academics worry about that!"

As he sailed across the lobby, floated through the revolving doors, and left the hotel, Urban ordered a double espresso from the flawlessly groomed waiter and sat back in the couch. Buckley was, as much as she hated to admit it, right. This solution worked for everybody. To be sure, the truth about the Red Army's barbaric behavior in post-war Berlin would remain buried, but that was just a continuation of the status quo and she had to admit that the forces pushing against full disclosure were simply too strong. The problem wasn't the Russians or even the German government and political elites. It was the people. We were still much too cowed by the war; we were still much too intimidated by the incessant flood of revelations about German crimes; we were still much too ashamed of what we had done and of what we had failed to do for us to be able to endure—and least of all initiate—a frank discussion of all the dimensions of the war. That crazy Eichendorf woman had a point. We had to be as guilty as possible, all of us, and we had to face total rejection. Only then, once we had experienced complete humiliation and could honestly say we had atoned for our mortal and venial sins, would we be in the position to talk about the sins of others.

The Russians were obligated to do the same. Their sins were probably as many and as mortal as ours. The rapes were only the tip of the iceberg. But penitence for Russian crimes was up to the Russians—and their non-German victims. The Poles, the Balts, the Ukrainians, the Jews—all had a right to excoriate the Russians for their silence. We didn't—in any case, not just yet. Close to two million German women had been brutally assaulted and raped after war's end. They cried for justice, but there would be and could be no justice because they were German. It was that simple. Justice was selective. It always had been and it always would be. Justice was also victor's justice. Losers always paid the price for their crimes, while winners did not. We lost—deservedly. The Russians won—undeservedly. Even so, they were the winners and we were the losers. And the two million women—and the five women among them—were losers who did not deserve to be heard until all of Germany's crimes had been atoned for. At least, unlike their men, the women hadn't been deprived of life. That was, perhaps, something to be grateful for. She drank her coffee and paid the bill. The waiter winked at her; she winked back—but distractedly, as her mind was elsewhere. One last conversation with Romanoff would be good. She asked the concierge to announce her coming and boarded the gilded elevator to the ninth floor.

*

Romanoff opened the oak door, his face beaming with unconcealed delight and a glass in his hand. He ushered Urban into his suite and, and excusing himself for celebrating this early in the day, offered her a seat and a drink. She declined. His suitcase lay on the bed and he was obviously in the process of packing. The drama was over and there was no reason for him to risk further scandal by staying in Berlin any longer.

"It's back to Cambridge for me," he said, as he made himself comfortable in a chair opposite her. "To be frank, I can't wait to leave this damned city."

"I quite understand."

"But, all's well that ends well, I suppose." He stole an ambiguous look at her. "How can I help you?"

"I feel a bit guilty," Urban confessed. "If it weren't for my interview, none of this would have happened."

"Yes, it's funny, isn't it? That our perfectly innocuous conversation and one or two photos should have unleashed such a maelstrom." He turned philosophical. "The ancients would have called it fate, but I prefer to think of it as an unfortunate confluence of events—an accident."

"The role of tragic hero fits you better, professor."

"Perhaps, but tragic heroes never end well. In the end, they are always guilty of something—even if they know not what—and must go down. I think," he continued after a moment's hesitation, "I prefer to be neither tragic, nor heroic, nor guilty, but just a simple professor, a simple historian dedicated to unearthing the truth about the past."

Reminded of her conversation with Buckley, Urban said, "Funny, I had just spoken about truth with an acquaintance. He thinks it matters only to academics, not to the real world."

"Your friend is right. Truth is our bread and butter. The world, on the other hand, rotates on the axis of convenience and interest. Truth usually gets in the way of those."

"Did truth get in the way of your convenience and interest, professor?" He would be evasive, she knew, but she had to ask the question.

"No, fortunately, in my case, there was a perfect alignment of the three. I have," he grinned, "absolutely nothing to hide and I wish only to return to my research."

"We all have something to hide, don't we? Did you know my father was a Nazi engineer? No, of course you didn't. Few people do, because I refrain from telling them. I hide that part of my past because it would be grossly inconvenient for me if the world knew that one of the *Berliner Zeitung*'s star reporters grew up with portraits of Hitler and huge swastikas adorning our living room walls. What's your dirty little secret, professor?"

It occurred to Romanoff, as he considered how he should respond as truthfully as possible, that most people were usually unwilling to accept the unvarnished statement of the truth as true. He knew that from his work on Rasha. The documents were indisputable. His findings were conclusive. And yet, troglodytes such as Ivanov refused to accept the manifestly true as true, because—and here Urban was definitely on to something—it was either inconvenient or opposed to their interests. In Ivanov's case, the calculus was simple: if Romanoff was right, then Ivanov was wrong. And vice versa. He decided to test his hypothesis.

"What if I were to tell you that I am a Soviet agent of influence and that I committed unforgivable war crimes during the war?"

"I'd say you were trying to create a smokescreen." The hypothesis had been confirmed! thought Romanoff.

"In that case, I won't say it," he said. "But I will say something almost as damning. I killed Germans—I should say very many Germans—during the war and most of the time there was nothing honorable, noble, or delicate about the killings. A gun to the head and bang. Are you following me?" he asked insistently. "They had surrendered and we lined them up and rewarded them with bullets in their skulls."

"It was, well—it was war," she mumbled, not having expected such a straightforward assertion.

"I know it was war!" he cried angrily. "I was there. You weren't. No woman was..." His voice, though bitter, had diminished to a whisper. "Count yourself lucky that only men have to kill and be killed, while you can dispatch us to the front with your lace kerchiefs and frilly bonnets."

"I don't know what to say." She was, he saw, on the defensive.

"And I saw rapes." She remained silent. "Do you understand what I am saying? I saw rapes, but I did nothing to stop them."

"It was—" she began.

"—war. Yes, I know." He spoke viciously and, in all likelihood, truthfully. "Do you know what that makes me?" Again, silence. "It makes me complicit—not guilty, but complicit. *That*," he spoke with a triumphant note in his voice, "*that*, my dear *Frau Urban*, is my—how did you put it?—dirty, little secret. Yours," he sniffed, "is commonplace, almost banal."

"It was war," she said weakly.

"Yes, it was war and all of us, all those who took part in the fighting, are killers. Pardon me, *were* killers." He spoke rapidly, brutally, almost violently.

"It was"—the words were almost inaudible—"war."

"Is there anything else?" His voice had turned mellow again and he appeared to show genuine concern for her emotional state.

"No, no," she whispered, "I think I know everything now."

"The truth?" He couldn't resist a self-effacing smirk.

"What passes for it." She shook his hand and, feeling emotionally exhausted and morally spent, headed for the door and exited the suite.

*

It was someone in Bonn, probably in the office of the Minister of Foreign Affairs, who decided that the best way to place a cross on the scandal and contain all its repercussions was to arrange for Professor Romanoff to depart for the United States in the same plane as the five women who had charged him with rape. The van would pick them up, along with Sieglinde Bollow and Gisela

Urban, drive them to the Kempinski, where they'd meet the professor in the lobby and hold a brief press conference, and then take them all to Tegel, where they'd board the plane for Bonn and the connecting flight to New York. If the first press conference went well, they could do a repeat performance at the German Information Center in New York and then in Bonn upon their return.

They'd kiss and hug before the cameras and, with all the media attention focused on the women and the professor, everyone would conveniently forget the core issues that no one knew how to address—the victimization of Germans and the criminal behavior of the Russians. Everyone would be happy. The Germans could go on pretending that they had only been perpetrators; the Soviets could go on pretending that they had only been victims; and the Americans could go on pretending that they had behaved impeccably before, during, and after the war. The women would go on a first-class junket in the land of the free and the home of the brave, Urban and Bollow would get a lot of free exposure in the media, and the professor would crawl back into his archives in Cambridge, Massachusetts, and, one hoped, never darken Germany with his shadow.

The bureaucrats were unreservedly delighted with their clever resolution of a festering problem. None of the actual participants in the trip was. The women were aghast at having to share a van and a plane with a man who might have been their assailant. Even though the evidence appeared flimsier with every day and their doubts surpassed their certainties, the whole affair—and Romanoff as its embodiment—made them feel queasy. Romanoff's enthusiasm for the enterprise was equally understated, though he appreciated that a photograph of him with them would spell his final victory. Bollow and Urban resented being dragged into an affair that both had believed was over for them. They even told the Ministry what they thought of the idea, but the officials at the other end of the phone line assured them that everything would go smoothly, reminded them that the Minister—and the Chancellor—would be grateful for their cooperation, and hinted at the possibility of some undefined rewards. Besides, it was possible that they might get a story or two out of the trip—something routine about American historical amnesia, pop culture, or oversexed social mores. All in all, they all grumbled, but held their noses, and decided to make the best of a bad situation.

The press conference in the lobby went well, much to everyone's relief. One reason may have been that they were all coached on what to say. Another was that the Ministry had cajoled several pro-government journalists into attending and asking easy questions.

"What have you learned from this affair?" one asked.

"To place my Christian beliefs above all else," one of the twins responded.

"What are your feelings toward these five women now that your ordeal is over?" another enquired.

"We all make mistakes and thank God that the press didn't focus on my academic whoppers!" Romanoff laughingly replied.

"Are you planning to write a book about this case?" a third journalist asked Bollow.

"No, the case is closed and there are more important issues bedeviling the country—such as atomic energy and world hunger."

"What's your view of Russia?" someone turned to Urban.

"It is a peace-loving country and détente is imperative. What's the alternative? Nuclear war?"

When a long-haired journalist began asking a long-winded question that seemed to be getting at war crimes and guilt, the Ministry official who handled the conference apologetically cut him off on the grounds that they had to get to Tegel as soon as possible—which happened to be more or less true. The journalist growled, but, with spirits high and patience thin, everyone rushed out and spilled into the waiting van.

*

What a joke! Sieglinde Bollow thought. *"Was für ein Witz!"* We

Germans are impossible—*unmöglich*. We live in an unreal world of delusions and illusions and pretend that the rest of humanity shares our hallucinatory lifeworld. Small wonder that we started two world wars and slaughtered millions in our crazy pursuit of that unreal reality. The best one could say was that other nations also preferred falsehood to truth. The Russian penchant for self-delusion was especially pronounced, but were the English, French, Italians, and Americans far behind? It was no surprise that this scandal ended the way it did—with a whimper. The professor was probably innocent and the women were probably mistaken, but no one cared about the balance of evidence. Their only concern was that the case conform to their delusions and illusions. We and the Russians were best friends and the Russians had liberated us. There was no place for Russian rape and German victimization in such an account.

And the rights of the women mattered not a whit—to anyone, whether male or female. The ultimate irony was that the main players in Romanoff's drama were, like me, women. We should be kicking and screaming and insisting that rape is never justified, never permissible; instead, the weight of our history and the need to sustain the extant story of German evil and Russian good prevents us, and will continue to prevent us, from telling the truth or, more accurately, the whole truth. Was not a partial truth a kind of lie? If so, then we Germans were as mendacious today as we were in the days of the Hitler regime. All that changed was the bit of truth that we concealed. She laughed bitterly. Well, at least we Germans have changed the nature of our lie. That was more than could be said about the Russians, who continued to believe what they had been force-fed by Stalin. Was that progress? Of sorts, she decided: something, however small, to be grateful for, however minimally.

She sat next to Urban in the second row. The professor climbed into the front seat next to the driver. The women and their handler, the Ministry official, occupied the seats in the back. Everyone was smoking, probably to avoid conversing. What was there to say? They all knew they were part of an elaborate charade. I have to pretend to respect and admire people who almost destroyed me, thought Romanoff. We have to pretend to respect and admire a man who may have tried to destroy us, thought the women. We have to pretend to respect and admire a political process that is destructive of what we journalists are supposed to reach for—the truth, thought Sieglinde and Gisela.

The van made its way down the Kurfürstendamm. Traffic was heavy, so progress was slow, but, contrary to what the official had said during the press conference, they had ample time to get to the airport. Swarthy workers in orange uniforms and white helmets were laying fresh asphalt on a piece of the avenue, at the point where it intersected Bleibtreustrasse. All the vehicles moved dutifully into one lane and crawled forward. The pedestrians waited dutifully for the light to change. The smiling mannequins behind the storefront windows dutifully displayed the latest fashions. A flock of gray pigeons, almost indistinguishable from the sky, fluttered above the tram wires, adding a welcome element of dynamism, of life, into the depressingly static picture.

Recalling the blown tire on his way from Tegel, Romanoff for a panic-stricken moment actually thought, as they stopped for the red light, that they made an ideal target for a terrorist attack—though why anyone would want to attack a van full of unimportant civilians wasn't clear. His anxiety attenuated by that rhetorical question, he decided he needed human company, turned to Bollow and Urban, and, after scratching his head in what he hoped would be interpreted as a disarming fashion and smiling as sincerely as possible, began saying, "Wouldn't it be a really savage irony if—."

He never completed the sentence. The missile struck the side of the van and produced a loud explosion followed by a raging fire. Survival was not in the cards for anyone that day, except for the driver, who only lost a leg and a hand. That same day, the Revolutionary Red Army Faction sent a statement to all the media outlets, in which it claimed that all Nazi collaborators and anti-Soviet traitors deserved to die and that further explosions would follow if Comrade Barbara Eichendorf was not released within seventy-two hours.

*

The American Embassy announced it would provide whatever assistance the Germans requested in tracking down these heinous cowards. The Soviets also extended their sympathy and offered to help. In reality, both sides were relieved that all traces of the embarrassing affair had finally disappeared—literally. *Frauen für Frieden* held a special evening dedicated to the peace-loving work of their five members. Urban's and Bollow's editors published extensive obituaries. Harvard produced a lengthy press release celebrating Romanoff's life and work and immediately started a search for an adequate replacement. Skriabin regretted that a valuable asset had been lost. Ironically, only Ivanov, abruptly bereft of his main competitor of so many years, felt genuine sadness at Romanoff's untimely demise. He would have preferred to have silenced him with the force of his arguments. He penned an article about Romanoff for the newsletter of the Russian Studies Association in which he pulled no punches and observed, much to his colleagues' consternation, that Romanoff was a "scoundrel and a cheat, but a damned smart one." A few weeks later, the Rashan Studies Association wrote that "only a scoundrel would call a dead colleague a scoundrel" and hailed Romanoff as a "giant."

The bodies, or what remained of them, were cremated and a funeral service was held at the crematorium. Several journalists, a few members of *Frauen für Frieden* all dressed in t-shirts with peace symbols, two of Romanoff's German colleagues, professors Schmidt and Bethmann, and a stocky gentleman with a severe crewcut, Colonel Lermontov, were in attendance at the brief ceremony. Schmidt and Bethmann delivered fulsome eulogies to Romanoff, with both calling him a "pathbreaking genius." Two journalists made a few anodyne remarks about Urban and Bollow and their commitment to "honest journalism." Finally, one of the *Frauen für Frieden* women praised the five women's dedication to peace. Lermontov, who happened to be in Berlin that day on other business, stood to the side and watched what he later told his comrades was a "disgusting display of insincerity."

For several months thereafter, German government officials pursued the idea of building a small monument to commemorate the victims of this tragic terrorist act. There were two main points of contention. Where should it go? Definitely not in the middle of the Ku'damm, on that they all agreed. But where, then, should it be placed? No answer was satisfactory. In some park? That seemed pointless. Near the Memorial Church? That bordered on the sacrilegious. Near the Wall? But the Communists weren't implicated in the terrorist act. The impasse might have been overcome with an anodyne plaque on the Free University's campus had it not been for the inconvenient question raised by some minor official: if they honored the victims of this attack, shouldn't they retroactively honor all the victims of past attacks? How far back in history should they go? Hitler? Bismarck? Napoleon? Friedrich the Great? Or, perhaps, the Romans?

Infinitely more difficult was finding agreement on the inscription. Everyone agreed that the only two things the eight victims had in common was their checkered relationship with the Nazi past and the Russian rapes of May 1945. No self-respecting monument could ignore that relationship and avoid mentioning Russia's ignominious role. The left-wing press at home and abroad would take great delight in recounting the women's almost unanimous enchantment with Hitler and in accusing the government of comparing Soviet transgressions with Nazi war crimes and thereby relativizing and minimizing Hitler's genocides. The right-wing press would delight in the revelations of Soviet criminality and disrupt Bonn's efforts to promote Ostpolitik with East Germany, Czechoslovakia, and Poland and détente with the USSR. The French, British, Dutch, Italians, and Austrians would snicker at Germany's discomfiture and express their deep shock.

Since the Russians would also go ballistic, the officials agreed that the monument issue was best relegated to the back of some file cabinet in the basement archive where it would remain for the foreseeable future. The Chancellor was rumored to have noted that, "Naturally, we must come to terms with our past—that goes without saying, as everyone knows—but not with *all* our past and not all at once." Official Bonn agreed, *natürlich*, as did official Berlin and the Socialist Party chiefs, and, applauded discreetly by the Soviet Embassy, which praised Germany for its love of peace, they let the matter drop.

END

ABOUT THE AUTHOR

Alexander J. Motyl

Alexander J. Motyl (b. 1953, New York) is a writer, painter, and professor. Nominated for the Pushcart Prize in 2008 and 2013, he is the author of ten novels, Whiskey Priest, Who Killed Andrei Warhol, Flippancy, The Jew Who Was Ukrainian, My Orchidia, Sweet Snow, Fall River, Vovochka, Ardor, and Pitun's Last Stand. Vanishing Points is his first collection of poetry. Worries, his second poetry collection, is slated to appear in 2022. He has done performances of his fiction at the Cornelia Street Café and the Bowery Poetry Club in New York City. His artwork has been shown in solo and group shows in New York, Philadelphia, Westport, and Toronto and is part of the permanent collection of the Ukrainian Museum in New York and the Ukrainian Cultural Centre in Winnipeg. He teaches political science at Rutgers University-Newark and is the author of seven academic books and numerous articles. He is the 2019 Laureate of the Omelian and Tatiana Antonovych Foundation. According to Academic Influence, Motyl was ranked sixth among the "Top Ten Most Influential Political Scientists Today."